Readers wil̶ ̶ ̶ ̶ ̶ ̶ ̶ ̶ ̶ ̶ ̶ ̶
—*Kirkus Reviews*

Feuer's characters are rounded, complex people...
Both Leslie and Jeff are defined by their personalities
rather than by their physical disability. As both characters declare their independence from their parents
and experience sexual awakening, few readers will
think that anything about these two is disabled.
—*School Library Journal*

[Readers] will sympathize with Leslie's struggle for
independence and delight in Jeff's freedom and
acceptance.　　　　　　　　　　　—*VOYA*

Leslie's struggle to become an adult, though unique in
its particulars, will be familiar to many readers.
Unsentimental writing keeps the story moving briskly.
Her disability...is by no means the novel's sole focus.
Rather, it is one of many vivid, vital threads from which
this story is drawn.　　　　　　—*Publishers Weekly*

AN ALA BEST BOOK FOR YOUNG ADULTS
A NEW YORK PUBLIC LIBRARY BOOK
FOR THE TEEN AGE

ELIZABETH FEUER lives in Colts Neck, New Jersey. Her
first novel was *One Friend to Another*.

PAPER DOLL

Also by Elizabeth Feuer
One Friend to Another

PAPER DOLL

Elizabeth Feuer

AERIAL FICTION

FARRAR · STRAUS · GIROUX

To Mark, with deepest love

Copyright © 1990 by Elizabeth Feuer
All rights reserved
Library of Congress catalog card number: 89-46393
Published in Canada by HarperCollins*CanadaLtd*
Printed in the United States of America
First edition, 1990
Aerial edition, 1994

PAPER DOLL

CHAPTER · 1

BOBBIE WAS SUPPOSED TO CALL for me at 7:30 sharp, but, as usual for the first day back in school, she was late.

"It's all right, I'll walk you to the bus stop," my mother said. "Maybe she'll catch up."

She was putting the finishing touches on my lunch. She cut the tuna sandwich neatly in half and dropped a package of cupcakes in the bag for dessert. My father, sitting opposite me at the table, was hidden behind *The New York Times*. His bagel with cream cheese rested uneaten on his plate.

"It's only half a block to the corner," I said. "I can go myself."

"It's no trouble," my mother insisted. "I like someone to be with you the first day."

There's no use arguing with her. The things she's

afraid of aren't things that make sense, so you can't reason them away. I pushed my plate aside and swung my legs around to stand. My legs, I call them, but they're no more mine than my shoes are. The legs I was born with— or the better part of them, anyway—I was forced to leave behind on the New Jersey Turnpike, one icy winter day about ten years ago. Now when I say legs I mean prostheses, clever devices of foam and plastic and metal I strap to my knees each morning. They let me walk and climb stairs and go to school, and they don't even look too bad, from a distance. But up close is something else again. I yanked down the hem of my long skirt and smoothed my blouse. An outfit with classic good looks, according to my mother, but not what I'd choose if I had my druthers. I guess I'll never stop longing for tight jeans.

"Every year, that girl gets more irresponsible," said my mother. "She knows you depend on her. How can she be so thoughtless?"

"She gets flustered, that's all."

"She's a high school senior already. You'd think by now she'd know better."

I walked to the window for one last search. "I'm sure she'll come. Just give her a few more minutes."

"Why, so you can both miss the bus? Let Mrs. Canelli worry about her own daughter. You just make sure she gives you a hand on the trip home, all right? They're going to load you down with books the first day. I don't want you trying to manage by yourself." I nodded.

Actually, Bobbie has always been scatterbrained and late, especially when she's feeling pressured. The first day of school throws her in a tizzy—she races around dropping things, trying to figure where she put her pencils. And every year my mother says the same thing. Bobbie's irresponsible. Self-centered. And every year, sooner or later, Bobbie finds her way to the bus stop to help me on and off and give me a hand with my books.

My mother slipped my lunch in my knapsack and helped ease the pack over my shoulders.

"Victor, we're going," she called to the kitchen. "I'm walking Les to the corner."

His newspaper crumpled as he set it aside. "What, she can't manage a half a block?" He looked around absently. "Where's Bobbie?"

"Who knows? I'll just walk Les to the bus stop and come back. So she'll have a little company."

He shook his head. Then he came closer, held my chin, and kissed my forehead. "You've got a lesson today?"

"No. Next Wednesday. Mom thought I'd get too tired, the first day."

"Ah." He tousled my hair and glanced at my mother. "I'll be gone when you get back," he said to her. "And late tonight. There's a lot of paperwork at the store. Seven or seven-thirty."

"You want me to keep dinner?"

"No, don't bother. I'll eat it cold."

We stepped outside. My mother held my elbow to steady me down the two steps to the walk. She's never forgotten the time I fell off the stoop playing jacks and split open my forehead and needed three stitches. She never forgets any of the world's hazards.

We went along slowly. That's the worst thing about my legs, they're tiring. So much dead weight. A wheelchair's easier, but then you need ramps, and special access. It's a trade-off. We trundled along, past Bobbie's house, to the corner. There was still no sign of her.

"I was looking through your closet last night," said my mother, picking at a speck of lint on my blouse. "You could really use some new outfits for school."

"Some jeans," I said.

"Not jeans. Leslie, be reasonable, you can't wear tight pants. And if they're loose you'll look like Farmer Jones." She pulled the shoulders of my top to straighten it. "Anyway, I thought maybe I'd go to the store this afternoon and look for some new things for you. One of those over-size sweaters, maybe."

"All right, Mom, whatever you think."

Over her shoulder, I caught sight of Bobbie running toward us. She was tearing down the street full-tilt, her shoulder bag bouncing off her hip.

"She's here," I said.

She came up panting, her hand on her chest. "I looked out the window and saw you go by. I didn't know it was so late."

The corners of my mother's mouth pinched downward, but she turned, so Bobbie couldn't see. "All right, sweetheart," she said, bending me close for a kiss, "I'll go now. If I'm out when you get home, I'm at the mall getting some clothes for you. I'll be back before supper."

"Okay."

"Have a good day at school. Don't overtire yourself."

She turned and hurried back to the house.

"I'm sorry I'm late," said Bobbie.

"It's all right. I'm used to it."

Bobbie and I have been friends since we were three. She is one of the few people who remembers how I used to be, back when I could play ball and ride bikes. But that was long ago. Then came the accident, and sitting-down games, Monopoly and Scrabble and checkers and dolls. And then came—what? It's hard to say now, what it is we share. We exist. We've been, and we are. And yes, I'm grateful to her, because it was Bobbie who gave my mother the courage to send me to regular school. It's an amusing thought that this girl who can't remember where her pencils are could give anyone a sense of security. But big, gentle Bobbie was my sheepdog. No one dared tease me when she was around.

We only had to wait a couple of minutes for the bus. I climbed aboard, hanging on the railing, and Bobbie stood behind me in case I tripped. As soon as I was inside, before I'd found a seat, the bus lurched into motion and I nearly tumbled into someone's lap.

"That jerk. Why didn't he wait?" Bobbie grabbed my arm and pulled me upright. She guided me to a pair of empty seats and eased in beside me.

"It's a new driver," I said. "He didn't think."

A couple of kids murmured "Hi" to us. A few new ones stared. You'd think I'd be used to it by now, but somehow it doesn't get easier. I shoved my feet under me and looked out the window.

"So, are you all set for another fun-filled year?" said Bobbie. "The last, thank God."

"Oh, it's not that bad."

"Speak for yourself. Me, I can't wait to get out. Although what I'll do then, I have no idea." She sniffed. "While you're off at famous school, becoming a genius."

I laughed. She considers it a foregone conclusion that I have greatness ahead of me. She can't seem to grasp that there are thousands of kids around the country who can play the violin as well as me, and that I'll be lucky just to get into Juilliard, let alone be a superstar there. Her faith is unshakable.

"You want to meet at lunchtime?" she asked when we got off in front of the school. "By the lockers? We'll go to the caf together."

"And sit with Dottie and Celeste?"

"We've got to eat, don't we? Come on, don't be such a stick in the mud the first day."

"All right, all right, I'll see you then."

By noontime I was lugging a stack of printed matter weighing at least ten pounds. Bobbie shoved it in my locker and handed me my lunch bag.

"Still not braving the cafeteria food? That's wise. Come on, I told Celeste we'd meet them. They're saving a table."

Celeste and Dottie—more Bobbie's friends than mine—are Franklin Roosevelt High's gossipmongers extraordinaire. They can always be counted on to know who's going with who, where, when. I can only take small doses of such things, and so I usually duck out to the practice rooms in the basement instead, for a short session of violin. But I couldn't do that the first day of school. Bobbie would be mortally offended, she thrives on gossip. And really, the girls aren't bad—just silly. In fact, they're painfully thoughtful. When they saw us coming, they pulled out a chair and helped me into it.

"Hey Bobbie, hey Les." They nodded. "Here, sit down."

Bobbie flopped in a seat. "I've got to buy lunch. Les, you want anything from on line?"

"Just a drink. Any kind." She vanished into the crowd. The table conversation was already in full swing.

"For my money," said Celeste, "the best-looking guy in the school is that Carlson. You know the one I mean?"

"Oh, of course, you would like him. Mr. Universe. Lifting weights and watching himself in the mirror."

"So? What's wrong with muscles?"

"What's wrong with a mind? And his could just about fit in his jockstrap."

"Nope. No room. My mind got there first." They laughed.

This went on for a few minutes. I unwrapped my sandwich and began eating lazily. There was noise all around, the tables buzzing with conversation. In a far corner, someone was laughing wildly; boys at the table behind us talked baseball in a deep rumble. Bobbie returned and edged in beside me, elbowing room for her tray.

"So what did I miss?" she asked.

"Nothing. We were discussing the hot prospects for the fall."

"What?" Bobbie looked from face to face. "You're discussing football?"

"No, idiot. Never mind, we'll tell you later." Dottie turned to me. "How are you doing, Les?" she asked. "Did you go to that music camp again?"

"Yep. Still in day camp at my age."

"Come on, you love it."

Celeste cut in. "You know, Les, I really admire your talent. I took piano for exactly one year, and it was the worst time of my life."

"Yeah, she had to spend a whole hour a day without boys. Golly." Dottie shook her head. "Don't pay any attention to her, Les. You just do what you're doing."

"Yeah," said Bobbie. "And then when you're a famous concert violinist you can send her postcards from Paris."

"That's right." Dottie nodded. "And she'll brag how she knew you when. She can tell all her clients at the beauty parlor." They giggled.

At long last, the period ended. Bobbie and I went together to dump our trash.

"I really wish we could eat together sometime," I said. "Just the two of us."

"We spend lots of time together. We practically live next door. Anyway, what's wrong with Dottie and Celeste? They like you."

"Nothing's wrong with them. It's just . . . we have nothing to say to each other. None of the same interests."

"Neither do you and I, in case you hadn't noticed." I looked at her in alarm, and she squeezed my shoulders. "Never mind," she said. "It hasn't stopped us yet."

"No." I smiled back. But it was a chilly thought—that perhaps Bobbie and I wouldn't be friends either, if we met now. If we didn't go way back. It had been easier making friends when I was little. When the only interest you needed to share was in being kids.

"So what have you got this afternoon?" she asked, as we started down the hall. I checked my schedule.

"Math, gym—you know, that la-di-da stuff they have me do. I finish eighth period."

"Will you be all right?"

"Of course. For Pete's sake, Bobbie, you're as bad as my mother."

"Well, I have to be. I report back to her." She grinned. "All right, then. I'll meet you in the lobby after eighth. Give you a hand, if you need it."

"I won't."

"I know. Well, whatever. Catch you later?"

"Yep." And I watched her, my best and only friend, skip off down the hallway. Then I turned the other direction and headed for class.

CHAPTER · 2

WHEN I GOT HOME from school that afternoon, the house was empty. My mother had left a note on the table: "Gone to the mall. Back by 4." I went to the kitchen and got myself an apple and a wedge of cheese and sprawled out on the living-room couch to eat, enjoying the quiet. It's rare that I have real solitude. Sometimes it seems I've been chaperoned all my life—to school, to lessons—even to the bathroom, till I was eight or nine years old. But I'd only rested five minutes when the doorbell rang.

"Drat," I grumbled, and got up reluctantly. But then I saw who it was. "Stevie!" I shouted, and flung the door wide.

When my brother Steve comes into the house, it's like dapples of sun beneath the trees. Bright, flickery, never staying long in one place. In one way, Steve is like my father: he's tall, about six feet. But that's where the resemblance ends. My father is all bones and angles, with a shock of white hair that sticks out like a scarecrow's straw. But Steve is a mischievous boy, with a full lower lip and round cheeks, light sandy hair and hazel eyes. He drives an old blue Chevy convertible, and in summer, when the top is down, his skin freckles and peels in the sun. But even when he spends months outside, like he did this summer, he doesn't get hard or muscular. I wonder sometimes if he'll always look as if he's in high school.

He sat on the couch, right in the spot where I had been, and stretched his feet out on the coffee table.

"So," he said. "How's my baby sister?"

"I'm fine. Did you just get in?"

"Not quite. Yesterday. I went to the apartment first."

"Before you came to see me? Shame on you."

"Well, I was dying to see you, Leslie, but fear is stronger than love." He fished in his shirt pocket for a pack of gum and offered me a stick. I shook my head.

"Still worried about Daddy?" I asked. "What is it this time?" He shrugged, waved me off. "Anyway," I went on, "I'm glad you're back. I really missed you this summer. Why didn't you call?"

"There weren't any phones in the Grand Tetons. Actually, I didn't want to take the chance of Victor answering." He said the name as if it were in italics. "But I brought you something."

"For me? What?"

"Don't get excited, it's nothing big." He dug in his pocket again and held out his hand.

"A rock? You brought me a rock?"

"Don't think of it as a rock. Think of it as the wilderness. The Rocky Mountains. The vast American West."

"I'll treasure it forever."

"Well, I couldn't very well bring back Old Faithful. And I know I'd never have persuaded you to come with me. I have trouble getting you to go for a spin in the neighborhood."

"Now that's not true. I love to go riding with you."

"Okay, then, let's. The convertible's parked out front."

"Right now? Just like that?"

"Sure, what better time? It's a gorgeous afternoon, the sun is out. I thought maybe we'd head for the shore."

"Steven, I can't just pick up and leave."

"Why not?"

"For one thing, it's a school day. The first day, in fact."

"Right. And on the first day of school you can't possibly have homework."

"And how about Mom? She's out at the mall buying me clothes."

"Leave her a note. Why are you still letting her do that, anyway? Don't you ever graduate to picking your own stuff?"

"I don't have time to shop." It *is* a tremendous hassle. Into the car, out of the car, walking. It exhausts me just thinking about it. Wriggling in and out of clothes, easing them over the straps. The Velcro sticking to everything.

"Oh, well," said Steve, stretching, "I suppose it makes Mom feel useful, looking after you. Of course, she should have gone back to work years ago. But with you she's got the perfect excuse."

I turned my hands palms up. He was right, Mom should have gone back. She used to work in the store, helping at the counter and keeping the books. But since my accident she'd been home, ten years now. And Dad had twice the work.

Steve got up and sauntered to the window. He pulled aside the curtain and let in a bright strip of late-summer sun. "So," he went on, his back to me, "what do you think? You up for that drive, or not?"

"I'd really like to." I shook my head. "I have practicing, too."

"It'll only be an hour. Okay? I promise. I'll get you back by five o'clock."

It was too tempting to resist. "Okay, Stevie," I said. "Just give me five minutes to wash up."

I went to the bathroom and splashed cold water on my face. Some sixth sense, some tickle at the back of my mind, told me there was a reason for this ride. Something beyond the pleasure of getting out in the open air. I tried not to second-guess, in fact wished myself wrong. But Steve has a poor track record. There have been so many crises over the years, so many scenes. It's almost a gift he has, for getting on my father's nerves. With his notes from school and his C grades, his rock music and his Chevy, which he practically assembled out of raw nuts and bolts during his senior year. Even the way he laughs—giggles, I guess you'd call it—can stand Dad's hair on end. If only Steve would grow up and act his age, maybe then we'd have a little peace.

When I returned, he was already outside on the front stoop.

"All set?" he asked.

"Guess so." I locked up the house, and then, remembering suddenly, said, "Oh, darn, I forgot the note for Mom."

"Skip it."

"But she'll worry," I pleaded.

"Leslie, worrying does parents good. Your problem is, you don't worry them enough."

From our house in central Jersey, it's only about fifteen minutes to the shore. Steve pulled out and headed onto the Parkway. It was a beautiful afternoon, sunny but not hot. The wind ripped through my hair as we barreled along. I was consumed with curiosity, but it was too noisy and windy to talk. Then we turned off the highway and drove through a tacky little seaside town and down to the beach. Steve helped me out of the car and we climbed the ramp to the boardwalk.

I suppose there once was a primitive wilderness in this spot—dunes and sea grass and scrub. It was hard to imagine it now. Along the boardwalk, most of the joints were closed for the season. We walked slowly past the shuttered stands with their signs for fudge and salt-water taffy, past the honky-tonk arcades. Then we found a bench and sat facing the breakers, the only wild things in sight.

"Remember the first time I took you swimming?" he asked. "The summer after your accident. What were you—about seven or eight? It gave Mom heart failure."

"I remember." How could I not? Unbuckling the legs, feeling so suddenly light and yet so helpless. I was utterly stranded without them. But I never felt afraid with Steve there. I remembered how he carried me, cradled in his arms, out where the water was calm. With his hands so lightly supporting me, I floated free and graceful as a sea creature.

"I haven't been swimming in years," I said. "Guess I'm too big to carry."

"No. You just haven't found my replacement."

He leaned back on the bench and stared out at the sand. "Les," he said. "I'm leaving school. Dropping out."

"What?"

"Yeah. I was thinking about it all the time I was hiking and bumming around. I've decided."

"Oh God. Steven. Must you?"

"It wasn't a hasty decision. I gave it a lot of thought."

"I hope so. I hope you cooked up some good reasons. Daddy's going to want to hear them."

"I know. Just thinking about telling him, watching him pull his hair, gives me, like . . . diarrhea." He arched his back and massaged his shoulders, sent me a sideways glance.

"I wish you wouldn't," I said. "I really wish you'd reconsider. You're a junior already, you're halfway there. You've put so much time and effort in."

"Right, a junior. That means two whole years still to go. Can you imagine it, Les? Can you imagine two years at something you can't stand, you don't belong in . . . It could just as well be twenty years. I'll die."

"You won't."

"You know what I mean. I'll . . . wish I could. Les, I just don't belong there. I've tried my best, I just can't stand it anymore. To be honest, I'm close to flunking out anyway."

I sighed. "Daddy's not going to like it, you know. School is sacred for him. Have you thought about how you'll tell them? What you're going to say?"

"Not the details."

"What are you waiting for, inspiration? Stevie . . ."

"I'll think of something," he said irritably. "Just give me a chance, all right? I'll rise to the occasion."

"Yeah. Right." We sat quietly for a moment, and then he leaned against me, giving a gentle nudge on the shoulder. "Cheer up, Les," he said. "In your heart, you know it's for the best. I only went to college because *he* insisted. I'm hopeless when it comes to books, I can't concentrate for five minutes. It makes no sense for me to be in school."

And there you have it, Steve in a nutshell. The little digs he gives himself, the lies that let him off the hook and disarm my anger. "Oh, Steve," I murmured. "How can you keep saying that stuff? You're plenty smart enough. If you just buckled down, if you tried . . ." He shook his head. "Just because you're not interested in the dumb games people play. The good grades and the good college and the good job . . ."

"Yeah. It's called success. Go on and say it, it's not a dirty word. I'm sure Dad won't spare me." He leaned his head back and tried to tighten his mouth, but his round lower lip jutted out in a pout. "God," he said. "Can you believe I'm only twenty? I've already screwed up more stuff than most people do in a lifetime. Even that damn car of mine runs lousy."

"No! The Chevy?"

"Oh, I'll fix it."

He helped me up and I stood a moment facing him. "Stevie. You know, don't you, that I'll love you no matter what?"

"Yeah, I know." And he threw his arm around me so I could lean on him as we walked back to the car.

On the way home, my guilt set in. I should have left my mother a note, she'd be worried. The only hope was that she might not have returned yet. But I'd barely gotten my key in the front door when she swung it open.

"Leslie, where in God's name have you been? You leave without a word, couldn't you at least have . . ." Then she spotted Steve coming up the front walk. "Oh. I should have known," she muttered.

We followed her into the kitchen. She had salad things and potatoes spread out all over the counter, and she went right away to the cutting board and started chopping. When Steve tried to put his arm around her and kiss her, she shrugged him off.

"You I'm not surprised at," she said to Steve. "But I thought at least Leslie had a little sense."

"I'm sorry," I mumbled. "I just rushed out. I didn't think."

She dumped a batch of potatoes in the skillet. They sizzled in the hot fat.

"Can I do anything, Mom?" I asked.

"Just sit."

She jabbed at the potatoes with a long spoon. Steve, looking at me, let his hands rise and fall. He pulled up a chair beside me, stretched out his legs, and waited for her to soften.

Finally, she said, "So when did you get in, Steven? Did you have a good trip?"

"Oh yeah, terrific."

"You saw all those mountains? Those—what do you call them? At Yellowstone?"

"Geysers. Yeah, those too." He pantomimed an eruption with his hands, raising his eyebrows at me.

She covered the pan and went back to the cutting board to fix the salad. "How was school, Les?" she asked.

"Okay."

"Bobbie helped with your books?"

"It all went fine."

"Good. I got you some stuff from the mall, if you're interested. In the living room, a bag from Macy's. Steven, if you still like chocolate chip, there are cookies in the canister. Are you staying for dinner?"

"Of course. You don't expect me to miss one of your meals, do you? Oh yes, and before I forget, I brought something. For you and Dad."

She looked up momentarily from her work. "You're buttering me up. Steven, you didn't have to do that."

"What is it?" I asked. "Another rock?"

"Well . . ." Steve searched his inside jacket pockets, both sides, and came out with a small paper bag. "In a manner of speaking." He held it out to my mother. "They're both in there," he said. "One for each of you."

My mother, warring between curiosity and vexation, took the package. She pulled out a thin necklace, silver and turquoise, and held it up to her blouse.

"Steven, it's beautiful."

"There's a belt buckle for Dad. Same type."

"It's very thoughtful. I'm sure he'll . . . be impressed." She reached up and grabbed a fistful of his hair. "Why don't you kids run along then," she said quietly. "Go relax in the living room until dinner's ready."

We went. Steve sprawled immediately in front of the TV. But I was in fact tired, as my mother had said. I picked up the Macy's shopping bag and headed for my room. My bedroom is an extension at the back of the house—a den, really, connected to the kitchen by two shallow steps. Originally, my mother put me there so I could avoid the second-story climb. She never intended it to be permanent. But gradually it got fixed up for me, with a private bathroom, a sit-down shower, lots of closets—even a private entrance through the back yard. The only problem is the decor, which is more like a hunting lodge than a girl's bedroom. But there was no way to reconcile a stone fireplace with a canopy bed. Instead, there's a studio with bolsters that looks like a couch, and a dark blue-and-green floral spread, with drapes to match.

I curled up on the bed, facing the wall. After a few minutes I heard footsteps, and voices. Steve and my mother, talking—maybe discussing me. Sometimes he does that, tries to persuade her to give me driving lessons, for instance. To do more on my own. He reminds her that I'll be leaving for college next year, and if I'm so helpless as that, how does she expect me to manage? In fact, she checked everything out, all the special arrangements. I could have told Steve not to worry. But I was too comfortable in bed. Their voices rose and fell, and my head grew muzzy. I couldn't follow the words. In five minutes I was asleep.

CHAPTER · 3

When I woke up, it was dark in the room and smells of meat loaf and fried potatoes wafted from the kitchen. I stumbled upstairs. My mother was sitting by the television, watching the news and crocheting, and Steve was lying on the couch.

"You have a good nap?" she asked.

"Why didn't you wake me?"

"We don't mind waiting. Dinner's keeping warm."

I rubbed my eyes and brushed the hair from my face. "What time is it?"

"Quarter to seven."

I sat on the edge of the couch and stared at the TV. I still felt dazed and stupid with sleep. They were running some feature story about a woman who custom-decorates cakes to look like famous people, and it was so make-believe and silly it made me wonder if I was still dreaming.

"I knew you'd knock yourself out the first day at school," my mother said. "And then traipsing all over with Steven. You should use a little restraint, especially since your brother doesn't have any. You look exhausted."

"I'm fine, Mom. I'm just not awake yet."

She frowned. "Anyway, you must be hungry," she said. "Let's eat, I don't know when your father's coming home." She turned off the television. We went to the kitchen and Steve set the table while my mother put out the food. She really shouldn't have let me sleep so long. The meat loaf was leathery from sitting in the oven, and the green beans had split along the seams.

"Les, if you're so tired, maybe you should skip your practicing tonight," she said.

"No, I can't. I'll only have time for a short session as it is. And I have a lesson soon. I don't want Elli to think I've been loafing all summer."

"Leslie, I'm sure Miss Rosenzweig would never—"

"Just kidding, Mom, kidding."

We had chocolate pudding for dessert, and then I went to my room and took out the violin. But I'd barely begun work when I heard the front door thud. I put the instrument away and went upstairs to see my father.

"Hello, angel," he said, kissing the top of my head. But he was looking at Steve.

There's a dance the two of them do, a kind of minuet or waltz, with long pauses and slow steps. Forward, back, to the side; forward, back. My father leads, but they both know the routine, and each time it's the same.

"Steven." It was a statement, with a nod.

"Hi, Dad."

He came into the room. The rest of us were standing, but he sat. He has a favorite reading chair, with a lamp over the shoulder and an end table to rest the newspaper on. But this time he sat on the couch, his long legs folding like a music stand.

"You're so late," said my mother. "We waited as long as we could, but the children were hungry."

"I told you I had extra work at the store. Of course, I didn't know I'd be graced with my son's company."

"Steve just got in this afternoon," said my mother. "He stopped to see us before school."

"I'm honored to be a stop on the itinerary."

"Victor, don't start. Go wash your hands and eat, you'll feel better."

He got up stiffly and followed her out. Steve and I sat facing one another, the table between us. He leaned forward, his head bent low, his hands laced behind his neck.

"Don't go in," I said. "Wait till he comes back, he'll be in a better mood."

It doesn't take long to finish what Daddy eats. About ten minutes later he returned and sat next to me. Although he leaned against the cushions, his back remained straight and rigid.

"So I take it you liked the West?" he said. "All those sights. Your mother tried to tell me."

"Oh yeah, it was great. Of course, I didn't get all the way to California, just to the Rockies."

"Oh, is that all? Just to the Rockies. Rose, where did we go for that wedding, a few years back? Ohio? Farthest west I've ever been."

"You're an old fogy," my mother said from the doorway. "Always sitting at home. Why don't you learn from your son and take a vacation once in your life? Here, I brought you coffee."

He raised the cup and sipped loudly. " 'Take a vacation,' she says. Just like that. And what would I do with the store?"

"Close it. Two weeks wouldn't put us out of business."

"Thank you, Mrs. Rockefeller. Maybe you forgot we have a son in college and a daughter starting next year. Anyway, who needs to look at mountains? I don't see the interest." There was a clink as he set the coffee cup down.

My mother tried to change the subject. "It was Les's first day at school," she said brightly. "Maybe you forgot."

"I didn't forget. But I don't have to ask Les, I know she did fine. Steven—when does your school start? Next Monday?" Steve nodded. "I know the tuition's paid up," he went on. "And the rent. What about books? You need money for that?"

Now, I thought. It's the moment, tell him now. Steve's cheeks turned a delicate pink and his lips parted. "No, I don't think so," he murmured. "Thanks."

"What, no books? What are you going to do, use last year's?"

"I have some money left," said Steve. "Money from the trip."

"Your *own* money? I am impressed." My father spread his arms along the backrest of the couch. "I was surprised you made enough with that landscaper to pay for your trip. For your knapsack and gasoline."

"It doesn't cost much to camp." Steve hunched forward, opened the candy dish, and rustled the papers inside.

"Wait, I think I have some chocolate in the kitchen," my mother said.

"It's all right, don't bother," Steve began, but she was gone. He unwrapped a hard candy and popped it in his mouth.

"You're going to be a junior this year, right?" my father asked. "Don't you have to declare a major?"

"Yes. Majors have to be declared by second semester junior year." He sounded as if he was reading aloud from the college catalogue. He's losing it, I thought. For God's sake, why doesn't he talk?

"Well, then. What's your area of interest? Is there anything in the vast world of human knowledge you find worthy of your attention?"

Steve gulped his sourball. "I . . . humanities," he said, choking. "Or political science or . . . sociology. Probably sociology. That's the best."

"Sociology. What's that, exactly?"

"A kind of . . . social science. About . . ."

"Social *science*? Science is chemistry, physics. You mean this is like . . . history, or something?"

"Not exactly," he mumbled. My mother came in with a handful of Hershey miniatures and deposited them on the table in front of Steve.

"What are you doing, Victor?" she asked. "Giving him the third degree?"

"Not at all, I'm merely trying to grasp . . . Explain it to your mother, Steven. Maybe she can understand."

Steve drew a breath. He reached for the chocolate, but his hand jerked suddenly and the candy skated across the table to the floor.

"Sociology," he faltered. "I was trying to tell Dad . . ."

I couldn't stand it any longer. "If you don't mind," I said, "I think I'll go to my room and practice. It's past eight."

"What? Oh, Leslie." My father nodded. I got up and wiped my hands hastily on my skirt. "Of course, sweetheart, go. This doesn't concern you."

"Thanks." I glanced at Steve and saw him clamp his jaw. What am I supposed to do? I wanted to say. You're the one that blew it.

I went back through the dark kitchen to my room. My violin was tucked in its niche at the foot of the bed. In the afternoon, when I'd first come home, I hadn't felt like practicing. But now I hungered for my instrument. Words buzzed in my ears like an insect drone; only the music could rise above them. I lifted out the violin and tucked it gently under my chin. Order, I thought. Structure.

For years now, I've had the same practice routine, and I slipped into it without thinking. It is much like entering a house and finding things where you know them to be. I started with the long bows, slow and steady, to build my sound. Then I moved on to scales and arpeggios, bowing exercises and double stops and études. The sequence comforted me. Only when I was done did I turn to my music: my best-loved piece, the Bach Chaconne. It is complex and difficult, a maze of sound. I closed my eyes and lost myself in its slow, mellow singing, in feeling the stroke of the bow and the vibration of the strings. I don't know how long I played. When I opened my eyes, my father was standing in the doorway.

"Don't stop," he said.

"It's finished."

"Do a little more, for me." He came in and sat on the bed. I started the piece over, from the beginning, but it wasn't the same with a listener and I broke off midway.

"What's the matter?"

"It's hard to concentrate with you watching."

"You have to get used to having an audience."

"I know. But you're not an audience, you're . . ." I stopped. "I was thinking about Steve."

"Oh, Steve. That's what I came down here to forget."

He stretched and walked to the fireplace. With his toe, he tapped the iron screen and it bonged a soft metallic tone. "I suppose you think I rode him too hard, right? All that talk about school."

"Something like that."

"Or maybe you think I should have let it slide. All that baloney he was serving up. Sociology. It's just a word, he doesn't know any more about it than I do."

"He knew you wanted an answer. That's why he said it, to please you."

"A real answer would please me. Not some phony baloney concocted for the occasion."

I looked at my hands. Why didn't it hurt him, too, to see Steve that way? So cowed, so tied in knots.

"He thinks life is easy," said my father. "Who's going to show him the truth but me?"

He came back and sat beside me. With one finger he touched my violin. "That Bach you were playing," he said. "Did you know it was one of my favorites?"

"Yes. Mine, too."

"I always wished I could play it, but I was never that good. Of course, now—I don't think I could remember how to hold the violin."

I didn't know how to answer. I thought of his instrument, gathering dust on the top shelf of the hall closet. No one had touched it since Steve quit playing ten years ago. Daddy hadn't passed that violin on to me. I think he thought it was jinxed. He got me a new one.

"I'll go now, angel," he said. "I just came to say good night." He bent down and lifted my chin and looked for a moment right in my eyes. "God took from you with one hand and gave with the other," he whispered. "It's like a miracle to me, to hear such music in this house." He kissed my cheek and left, shutting the door lightly behind him.

I felt shaky. He loved me so much. Maybe he knew I was concealing something, lying for Steve. Oh, why couldn't they get along? I was like an electric relay station between them, buzzing signals and garbled messages back and forth. But what could I do? When they met face to face, the words sparked and flared and burned up the wires. I put my violin in its case and undressed for bed.

CHAPTER · 4

THE NEXT MORNING BOBBIE WAS on time for the bus, looking bright and shiny as a fresh apple. She was wearing a pale yellow sweater I hadn't seen before, and her long blond hair was wavy. I guessed she had gotten up early to curl it.

"You're looking stunning today," I said.

"Come off it."

"No, I'm serious, you look nice. What's the occasion?"

"Is it that unusual for me to look nice?"

"Bobbie, you know that's not what I meant."

For someone with basically nothing to complain about, Bobbie grumbles a lot. It's true she's on the heavy side, but so what? Her complexion is straight out of a Camay commercial, she has rippling blond hair long enough to sit on, and besides, a lot of guys like big boobs. "Boys love it?" she always says. "Well, then, where are they?" I tell her she's underappreciated and her day will come.

We found a seat together and I filled her in about Steve.

"Your dad's so rough on him," she said. "What's he so mad about, anyway?"

"I don't know. They've been like that as long as I can remember."

"What do you suppose your father will do when he finds out? I mean, when Steve finally tells him he's dropping out of school?"

"To tell you the truth," I said, "Steve is so scared, I'm not sure he will tell. My dad'll probably find out when the college stops sending bills."

For the rest of the trip, we sat thinking our private thoughts. But as we prepared to get off the bus she said quietly, "I notice you brought your violin. You, uh, have something on today?"

"Oh. That." I hated to tell her. But there was no need, she was too quick for me.

"Oh, Leslie," she groaned. "You're not going to practice at lunchtime, are you?"

"Well, I . . ." I started to explain, about my audition being just around the corner, and how much I needed the extra work. I gave up midway. "Maybe you could join me sometime," I ended lamely. "Bring a sandwich and listen."

"What, down in the basement? I don't think so."

It was a nice way of putting it. She wasn't refusing, it was the school that wouldn't allow it. It was my privilege, not hers, to use the practice rooms during lunch and to travel the halls at off-hours. My bonus for being handicapped, and talented. It was nice of her to frame it that way, instead of saying what was also true, that she loved her time with Dottie and Celeste, preferred their chitchat to my music. She was tactful, my Bobbie. But, then, I didn't say what I thought, either. That her friends were shallow and silly and a waste of time. Much as they tried to be nice.

"Well . . . I guess I'll see you in the afternoon, then. After school. Right?"

"Yep."

And so at lunchtime I took my peanut-butter sandwich and Oreos down to the practice rooms. It felt good to work out; I hadn't had much time yesterday. I did an abbreviated warm-up and then worked on my Brahms. Lost myself in it. It's a constant source of disgruntlement to my teacher, but the fact is, what I like best about the violin is practicing. I know that sounds strange, most students dislike practicing and most teachers wish students would do more. But for me the great joy of music is making the sounds. Thinking, analyzing, working out musical problems. I even enjoy scales. The pity is, you can't make a career out of playing for yourself. Sooner or later you have to get up in front of people, and that's where my trouble starts. It's not just stage fright, either— the shakes, I mean. There are pills now that you can take for that. It's more the idea of being on display and being judged. Everything is fair game, from your dress to your technique to your ideas. Did you understand this piece? Did you do it justice? And there's the flip side, too: Did the audience understand it? Are they capable of taking in what you're trying to say? Because music is a language, and classical music, I sometimes think, is Greek. People always seem to want to hear the pieces I like the least,

the show-off stuff—Sarasate, Paganini. They don't realize that the Bach Chaconne is twice as difficult, not to
mention ten times as deep. I get frustrated. And the result
is, I don't do many recitals, I don't get enough experience,
and I cause my teacher to worry. I would see Elli next
week, for the first time since June, and I knew already
what she would say.

I got too deep into the Brahms and didn't realize it was
time to quit until the bell rang. What I should have done
then was to wait for the second bell and go to class late.
They always excuse me. But I didn't think. I just headed
upstairs, like an idiot, into that jam-packed hall, and by
the time I realized my mistake I couldn't do anything
about it. It's difficult for me to cope with crowds, I'm slow
and my balance is precarious. I cautiously made my way
to the edge and walked with one shoulder brushing the
wall. Then, out of nowhere, I felt a jolt—hard, like being
clipped by a motorcycle. My feet went out from under
me. I tried to grab onto something—I knew I was going
down—but the surface of the wall was smooth and glossy
and there was nothing to catch hold of. I tumbled backwards, with my right arm wrenched underneath. I never
even saw who did it.

My first thought was for my violin, but it was fine, tight
in its case. My backpack, however, had skidded across
the hall; also my shoulder hurt. A couple of people bent
down to help.

"Can you get up?" said one of them. "Are you all
right?"

"I think so." The waxed floor was slippery. They
grabbed me on both sides and eased me to my feet. Someone brushed me off in back.

"You okay?" asked a boy.

"Yes, fine," I said, irritable from being awkward and helpless. "I'm fine, you can go."

"You sure? He bashed you pretty hard. I think you'd better see the nurse."

"I'll take her," said a voice behind me. It seemed a whole committee had organized to see to my welfare.

I turned. The voice belonged to the scrawniest example of male adolescence imaginable. He barely looked capable of supporting his own weight. Then, as I took a closer look, I realized the boy had cerebral palsy. I'd met kids with CP before, at the rehab hospital. He stood by the wall, hugging his books, his bony elbows jutted out, his legs bent and pigeon-toed.

"No, I'd better," said another boy grudgingly. "She might need some help."

"Well, I'll come along. I can stay with her, I've only got study hall now."

We waited until the crowd cleared and then set out together to the nurse's office. We were a ludicrous little band, inching along—me with my slow, stiff walk, my new comrade teetering alongside like one of those clown toys that kids try to knock over and can't. His feet went swoop, swoop, making circles on the tile floor. The third musketeer, the normal one, walked between us with his eyes straight ahead, as if he could catch what we had if he stared at us. Come to think of it, even he walked funny. Maybe it was an effort for him to go so slow.

"You think you'll be okay if I just leave you here?" he asked when we reached the infirmary. "The nurse must be out to lunch or something, but she'll probably be back soon. You can wait on the chair here."

"Thanks for helping me. I'll be fine."

" 'Cause I gotta run, I'm late for math."

"I'll stay with her," my companion volunteered. My knight.

We sat down on a couple of hard chairs. I glanced at him from the corner of my eye. He would have been funny-looking even without CP. He had a mop of red hair almost as long as a girl's, and the kind of white skin that most people have only on the insides of their wrists or under their bathing suits. His face was spattered with freckles.

"I've been wanting to meet you," he said. "I'm Jeffrey Penner."

"I'm Leslie Marx."

"Yeah, I know. The guidance counselor told me about you, before I started this year. I just transferred from Pennsylvania. I guess she figured it would make me more comfortable, knowing I wouldn't be the only freak in the joint."

"Is that how she put it?"

"No, of course not. She said, 'Er, ahem, mumbledy-mumbledy, of course, you understand.' I was just translating."

My irritation rose. If he wanted to call himself a freak, that was his business. But he could leave me out.

"Sorry." He cut in abruptly. "I know, I have a crude sense of humor. It's part of my elaborate defense system. I didn't mean to be obnoxious." He cleared his throat. "The guidance counselor said you were brilliant. A musical prodigy, something like that."

"Hardly. I just play the violin."

"Oh, my goodness, don't tell me you're modest, too.

Don't you know that's out of fashion? Nowadays you're supposed to brag. I would, if I could do anything."

"I'm sure you have your talents." Starting with an adhesive perseverance, I thought.

"Really, I don't. I mean, nothing special. But you fill me with admiration. Not to mention passion, but I'm too shy to talk about that." He paused a moment for breath. "That guy really clobbered you, didn't he. He didn't even look where he was going."

"It happens."

"I know. All the time, to me. Of course, I'm so spastic I can drop my books perfectly well on my own. I don't think it's because of the CP. I've got a very mild case— just my legs, really. I can talk just fine—too much, according to most authorities. But I am a klutz. When I was a kid, I used to toss my books in the air sometimes. Just for a change. All those little homework papers, floating down like confetti."

In spite of myself, I smiled. There was something appealing about the image of young Jeff in a paper snowstorm. At least his dumb joke was at his own expense.

At that moment the nurse came in.

"Why, Leslie, Jeff. What are you two doing here? Are you all right?"

"I am," said Jeff. "I'm keeping Leslie company. Some moron knocked her down in the hall."

"Oh, dear. Are you hurt anywhere?" She made a quick survey, checking for broken bones. She held my head and turned it from side to side.

"I'm all right, really. Just shook up. And I twisted my shoulder a little."

"You sure?" And she knelt down to look at my legs. Why, oh, why, do they always look at my legs? You can't hurt plastic. If they broke, I'd need an engineer, not a nurse. But she poked around anyway, straightening and turning, while I sat there rigid, with the flush creeping upward from my neck to my ears to the roots of my hair. Couldn't she at least have taken me in the examining room? Away from this . . . Jeffrey, this total stranger, this *clown* . . . But then I glanced at him and saw he had his back to me and was giving minute attention to the empty hall. I felt a rush of gratitude.

"I think you're all right," the nurse said. "But maybe it would be best for you to go home. I'll call your mother to come get you. Do you think she's in? Jeffrey"—the nurse turned to him—"why don't you go sit by my desk now? I'll write you a late pass. It's so nice you two met, although the circumstances . . . Jeffrey, are you listening?"

He turned back toward her. "Oh, yeah. Sure." He gave me a ghostly wave of the hand. "I'll see you round, Leslie. Okay?"

"Yeah."

The nurse walked me to the main office and told the secretary to dial my mother.

"She's fine, I'm sure. But Mrs. Marx will want to be told."

Thinking about my mother gave me a headache. I knew just what would happen. A trip to the doctor, an afternoon of fussing and worry and recriminations. When I get cut, my mother bleeds. But there was no stopping the nurse. Schools are scared to death of kids with medical problems, afraid they'll be sued if anything goes wrong. The secretary dialed my mother and in fifteen minutes—no, ten—she was by my side.

"Leslie, what happened to you? Are you all right?"

"I'm fine, Mom. I just fell."

"Some boy jostled her in the hall," the secretary said. "He wasn't watching where he was going. The kids aren't as careful as they should be, sometimes."

"Did you see who did it, sweetheart?"

"I have no idea."

My mother turned to the secretary. "I'll want to bring this up with the principal," she said. "The school should be taking some extra care, you know? Making *some* provisions . . ."

"We're very sorry it happened, Mrs. Marx," the secretary said. "But you have to understand this is a regular school. We don't have the resources to make special arrangements."

"Mother, I'm all right," I said. "It could have happened to anyone. You don't have to make such a big deal."

She turned back to me. "And you don't have to be so cavalier, young lady. Are you sure you can walk? Because I brought the wheelchair, just in case."

"My legs are fine, Mother. The only thing I hurt at all was my shoulder."

"Which shoulder?"

"The right one." Immediately I regretted telling her. Because the next words she said were: "Then maybe you'd better skip the practicing for tonight. You know how you overdo it. And, anyway, there won't be much time after you see the doctor."

"Mother, I don't need to see the doctor, I . . ."

"And where's your medical diploma? Leslie, it's best to check it out."

"All right, all right." There was no point in debate.

It was close to six when my mother and I dragged

home. According to the doctor, I had a black-and-blue mark on my shoulder that would be gone in three days. According to my mother, that meant I needed three days of rest. No practice. Even my father can't make headway against her when she's protecting her children's health.

"What's the difference if she misses a few sessions?" I was listening from my room; her voice came clearly through the walls. "She's got the rest of her life to play violin."

"But only a few months to get ready for Juilliard. What's the matter with you, Rose? You treat her like she's made of eggshells. Every little hangnail, you think she should stay in bed a week."

"And what about you? You think she's got nothing else to do but play music. She's a young girl, Victor, a seventeen-year-old girl. She can't be working every second."

I rolled on my side and pulled the pillow over my head. Oh, how I wished I could play. How I wished I could tuck the violin under my chin and let the music fill my ears, drowning out everything else.

CHAPTER · 5

THE INJURY TO MY SHOULDER was slight, and it healed quickly. The next week I was able to go to my lesson. And so my mother drove me to New York, as she had every week for the past ten years, and dropped me at my teacher's brownstone on the Upper West Side. My teacher, Elli Rosenzweig, has been guiding my musical progress since I was seven. She is a crusty, opinionated old lady, very tall and straight, who wears her white hair bundled on the top of her head in a severe knot, like an old-fashioned school principal. I can still remember how she terrified me the first time we met—firing off questions and fixing me with her clear blue eyes. Then she tried to put me at ease by giving me a chocolate bonbon out of one of her Waterford candy dishes.

"Go on, open it up, take one," she said, holding out the bowl. "What are you waiting for? We have a lesson to start here." She assumed I couldn't make up my mind which bonbon to choose, but in fact I was afraid to touch the glass dish. It looked as if it might shatter into a million priceless slivers. "Go on. If it's that hard for you to pick, take two." Her roughness only unsettled me more. She hates me already, I thought. Finally I opened the bowl, reached in, and took an opera cream. It wasn't until much later that I realized that no one offers Godiva chocolate to an enemy. And as for the glass trinket she had me hold—how better to show that she trusted my hands?

Over the years, Elli and I have developed the custom of beginning each session with a chat. Sometimes we discuss specifics—technique, repertoire—sometimes politics, art, or the state of the world. We have our occasional misunderstandings. But no matter how heated the conversation gets, the relationship itself is solid as a rock. And when I go away for a month or two, as I had this summer, I miss her. It was a pleasure once again to ring her bell and receive her kiss on both cheeks.

"So you're back," she said. "I trust you had a pleasant summer? Maybe squeezed in a little time to practice?"

"I always practice. You know that." It was a familiar tease.

"Somehow I imagined otherwise," said Elli. "This music camp in the countryside, with the green trees—I pictured more *Déjeuner sur l'Herbe*. What were you working on there? The Bach suites? And a Brahms sonata . . ."

"Yes. And the Mendelssohn. Still."

"Yes, naturally, the concerto. Well. I hope at least you haven't lost your technique in the treetops." She reached out a slender hand and took a cigarette from her silver box.

"Elli! I thought you were quitting," I said.

"I need at least one vice. And at my age the choices are limited." She tapped the cigarette and lit it. "Only one puff," she said. "Out of consideration for you." She inhaled deeply and said, "Now that you're returned, I assume your thoughts turn to your audition?"

Direct as always. "I had begun to think about it."

"Good. Thinking is the essential part. Without thought, practice is worthless. Mindless. Right?" She ground out her barely touched cigarette. "What do you think of your playing now?" she asked. "What are your strengths and weaknesses?"

I hesitated. "Well, my intonation's good, and my vibrato. Of course, my bowing always needs work . . ."

"Leslie, I was not referring to technical aspects. Where is your weakness psychologically?"

"What?" Then I saw where she was headed. "Please, Elli." I held up one hand. "Don't start, all right? I know what you're going to say. We've been through this a dozen times."

"A dozen times, a hundred times. So what? Leslie, music is made to be heard. You have chosen a performance career. And this, this audition, is the most crucial kind of performance. It's not enough, you know, for you to walk in there with a few little pieces prepared. I don't care how well you play in the studio; at an audition it won't be enough. A thousand violinists want to go to Juilliard. You must distinguish yourself. You must have stage presence. This is something you only learn by playing in front of an audience."

I sighed. Easy for her to say. Elli thrives on performance. She'd have been a concert violinist herself if she hadn't had to spend her youth fleeing Hitler. "Elli," I said. I spoke deliberately, as if she were a five-year-old. "Elli, I do play. I do recitals every year . . ."

"Recital. One. Singular. This is not enough. Remember, you are very inexperienced. Even your ensemble playing is limited."

"There was the Youth Orchestra. I played there for two years."

"When? Three years ago? And what about all the competitions you refused to enter?"

"You know that's not my fault." I gestured to my legs. "It's not exactly easy for me to travel."

Elli gazed at me with her clear blue eyes. "Leslie," she said quietly, "why do you do this? Why do you make all these excuses? A violinist of your quality should be glad to perform. To show off what you can do." I didn't answer. "Is it stage fright? You get nervous? Sweaty hands?"

"Not exactly."

"What then?"

I saw her sitting there, so straight, so perfectly controlled. She would never understand how I felt. The woman was iron. But no. She softened.

"Well, all right," she said. "I've done my best. You'll come to it when you're ready." She got up and went across the room to get her violin. "Let's start," she said. "Let me hear what you learned at that fine music camp of yours." And so we began. I'd won the battle. But victory over Elli was not a very satisfying experience.

With all our talk and catching up, it was late afternoon by the time we finished. I slipped on my jacket and went outside to wait for my mother. At the far end of Elli's block, I could see and hear the traffic of Broadway—the roar of cars and the beeping of horns. Just a few blocks downtown was Lincoln Center and the Juilliard School. I'd gone to the Philharmonic many times with my father. But long walks tire me. I'd never ventured down Broadway on foot. There was so much life there, so many fruit stalls and newsstands and restaurants. And I had always seen them from the car, through the haze of dust-specked windows.

A horn tapped out close behind me and my mother pulled up.

"How was your lesson?" she asked, as she opened the door for me. "What did Miss Rosenzweig have to say about your progress this summer?"

"Oh, she seemed satisfied. You know how she is, though. She doesn't gush."

"Did you play the whole hour and a half? You ran very late."

"We talked some."

"About what?"

"This and that. The audition. Recitals. She wants me to play more for people."

"That would be nice."

"Not for me, it wouldn't."

It came out harsher than I intended, and my mother's mouth snapped shut. I felt a twinge of guilt. It's so easy to silence her.

"Thank you for waiting," I added. "I hope I haven't made dinner late."

"It's no problem. I have everything prepared at home."

I turned on the radio, and for the rest of the trip we didn't speak. It was nearly dark when we arrived. My mother went direct from the garage to the kitchen to start heating supper, and I went to my room. I'd barely been there five minutes when the phone rang and my mother called me to pick up.

"It's Bobbie," she shouted. "I think she wants to come over."

"Would that be all right?" I stepped up to the hall and stuck my head in the kitchen. "Daddy won't be home for a while yet, will he?"

"What about your homework? Oh, well, go ahead if you want. But she can't stay long." Five minutes later, Bobbie knocked at the door to my room.

In contrast to the way she'd dressed for school recently, Bobbie today looked tired and bedraggled, in an oversized pink sweatshirt and baggy jeans. She wandered restlessly about the room, touching my books and tapes and pulling down the elastic of her shirt, while I stretched out on the bed and shoved a bolster under my head.

"So where have you been keeping yourself lately?" I asked. "Except for the bus, I've hardly seen you all week."

"That's not my fault. You stopped eating with us."

"I'm sorry. But I'm so busy practicing. With a little schoolwork thrown in for good measure."

Bobbie sat down at my desk and started to play with my pens and erasers.

"Schoolwork," she said. "I'm already flunking math. The term's hardly begun and already I'm lost."

"Don't be ridiculous. You haven't even had your first test."

"No, but I can tell, we handed in homework. Why do I have to take that stupid stuff, anyway? Trigonometry.

Who cares? In five years, no one will ever know the difference if I learned it or not."

"You don't want to flunk, though. You've got to graduate."

"Oh, I'll manage somehow. I just wish . . ." She bounced a pink eraser against the desktop. "Oh, never mind. What have you been doing?"

"I told you. Music. Nothing unusual. I had my first lesson with Elli this afternoon and we argued about recitals. I suppose I'll have to do some, but I really don't want to." But Bobbie wasn't listening. She was cradling her head in her hand. Then she looked at me.

"Les?" she said softly. "Les, do you think I'm stupid? Tell me the truth."

"I think it's a stupid question," I said.

"You're trying to wriggle out of it. That's not an answer."

"Why are you asking?"

"Oh, it's . . . I don't know. Yes, I do. You know Eric Kupmann? The guy who won the junior math medal last year?"

"It sounds dimly familiar. What about him?"

"I went out with him Saturday night."

A boyfriend. So that explained the new clothes. "Great," I said. "Where'd you go?"

"Leslie, he's brilliant. I mean, really smart. He kept talking all night about math, and college, and whether he wants to go to Harvard or MIT. Jesus. And I'm sitting there wondering if I'll be able to graduate. You know? I just couldn't figure out why he was bothering. What does he see in me, anyway?"

"You're a nice person. He probably likes you."

"Like fun. I'm a jerk. I acted like a baboon all night. 'Uh, duh, I don't know.' "

"I'm sure it was nothing like that."

"Then he asked me out again."

"No!" I shook my head. "Not another date? Gee, Bob, you've got a major problem here."

"Very funny." She got up and started to pace back and forth across the room. Finally she stopped and rested her back against my desk to look at me.

"Bobbie, I'm afraid I don't understand the difficulty."

"Well . . . I don't know how to explain." She took a deep breath. "I wasn't prepared."

"For what?"

"For him. For how he acted."

"What did he do?"

"Well . . . nothing. I mean, just the usual. Only more so. Les, we must have made out for two hours in his car. He undid everything. My bra, my pants . . ."

"That's not a first."

"But it was only our first date. And I'm not sure . . . I felt so tacky."

"Then why did you do it?"

There was pause.

"You'll laugh at me."

"I won't. When did I ever do that?"

She looked up sharply. "About thirty seconds ago. If you recall."

"Yes. All right. But I won't now."

"I was thinking," she began, "about whether it would help. Help him like me. You know what I mean? Because I wasn't sure, I mean, I sounded so dumb and all. And I really wanted him to ask me out again. God! It's pathetic, isn't it? Imagine Celeste doing a thing like that. But I want a boyfriend, Les. I want him to call, and . . . I'm not attractive like Celeste. So I compromise a little. It's not so bad, right? Not the end of the universe if some guy cops a feel."

I pushed myself up on my elbows. She was slumped against my desk, and her body, under her loose pink sweatshirt, was heavy and thick. But her skin was smooth as a rose petal, and with the gold hair flowing down her back she was like a Renaissance painting. Just this side of perfect.

"You know," I said in a level voice, "a lot of people would say that Eric Kupmann doesn't deserve all this consideration. All this weighty thought."

"What do you mean?"

"He's not gorgeous or anything. He's not class president or captain of the football team. He's just a smart kid with bad skin."

"Leslie! That's horrible. Besides, I'm in no position to pick and choose."

"Why not?"

"Because . . ." She gestured with an open arm, as if offering herself.

"Because you're not pretty enough? You don't have a twenty-four-inch waist? Well, where does that leave me, then? What do I have to do, hand out fliers? Write my phone number in the boys' room?"

For a long moment she didn't answer. "Did I ever talk about you like that?" she said at last. "I don't think that was fair, Leslie."

"Oh, you know I didn't mean it like that, but . . ."

"But what? What is it, Les? Don't I have rights, too?

Just because I'm not . . . brilliant." She broke off. I massaged my forehead with both hands. A minute passed before I could speak again.

"But, Bobbie. You said it yourself," I went on gently. "Forget what he thinks about you. You're not sure you like *him*. Why should you lower yourself if you're not even sure . . ."

I didn't get to finish the sentence. She rose and went to the outside door. "Bobbie . . ." I said weakly.

She turned. "I see what you think," she said. "I'm not *that* dumb. Leslie, we all know you're a very superior person, with your music, and your career. No time for dating, or nonsense like that. All right, that's your privilege. But it doesn't make you an authority on other people, Les. It doesn't give you the right to judge me."

"Bobbie, I wasn't. I only meant . . ." It was too late. She was gone, closing the door behind her with a muffled thud. I leaned back on my bed. How could it have happened so fast? We'd had our spats, but never like this. Never that final thud of a closed door. But, honestly. Why did she tell me things if she didn't want to know what I thought? Or was it only approval she was after? She seemed to think of me as some kind of impartial referee, always on the sidelines and so better able to see the plays. If she only knew how tired I was of listening to her insecurities about her looks. To her complaints about compromises I would be happy to make.

CHAPTER · 6

By mid-october, between practice and homework, I was in the full swing of the schoolyear. I was busy, but with both Bobbie and my brother making themselves scarce, my social life was rather grim. Even my father finally noticed me looking peaked.

"I thought you might like to come down to the store today, Leslie," he said one Saturday over breakfast. "Just for the morning, you know? Like you did when you were a kid."

"I have work to do. Practicing . . ."

"You can bring your homework along, work on the desk in back. And you'll still have time to practice in the afternoon." He managed to say the whole speech without looking up from his newspaper.

"Gee, Daddy"—I leaned forward in my chair—"I

haven't been to the store in ages. Will you let me play with the cash register?" It took him a moment to realize I was joking. "All right." I laughed. "Just give me a half hour to get ready."

Walking into my father's hardware store is like stepping into a time machine; instantly I feel about ten years old. It was my favorite place in the world when I was a kid. I love the smells, the paint thinner and potting soil and birdseed, and I love the bins of nails and washers and bolts. Nothing much changes in a hardware store—there aren't any fashions. There are always snow shovels in winter and garden hoses in summer. Up front is the key machine that fascinated me when I was little. I used to goggle at it as it worked, *kachunk kachunk kachunk*, biting out new keys exactly like the old ones. I would beg my father to run it for me, and he usually did. Eventually, I accumulated a whole boxful of useless keys.

Daddy and I drove down to the place just before nine. He unlocked and set up in front and I went to the back office and spread my books on the desk. Fred, the head clerk, came in and said hello, and I got busy on my history homework. I lasted about five minutes. Then, thinking math might be less stupefying, I fished out my book and looked for a pencil. I couldn't find one. So I started to search the desk, pulling open the drawers. I didn't find the pencil, but I found something else: a flat green cardboard box that looked vaguely familiar.

I pulled it out and opened it. It was mine, from when I was little. Inside the box were three paper dolls with names—Patty, Kim, and Roxanne—penciled on their backs. They were dressed beautifully—nicer than any real people I knew. Kim was in a bride's costume, and

Patty and Roxanne wore party gowns. There were lots of other clothes in the box too, a drum majorette's outfit, and a nurse's uniform, and lots of regular skirts and pants. They had all been used, but so lovingly that not a single outfit was torn or dirty.

"Daddy!" I called out. "Dad! Look what I found back here!" When he didn't answer right away, I peeked out and saw that he was mixing paint for a customer. While he rang up the sale, I carefully carried the dolls up front and began to set them up on the counter, fixing them in their plastic holders. It was a bit crowded, with the key chains and car deodorizers and all, but I shoved things aside to make room.

"Do you believe this?" I pointed. "Have you had these in the store all this time? I didn't even remember them."

"Well, you know how you used to play back there in the office. You must have left them. We found the box a few weeks ago when we were cleaning the storeroom."

"Why didn't you bring them home?"

He raked his fingers through his hair and it fluffed up. "You want to play with paper dolls? Aren't you getting a little old?"

"I know, but . . . these are pretty ones. I notice you didn't throw them out."

He started to mumble an answer. I picked up two of the dolls and danced them across the glass, which reflected their bright party gowns like a ballroom mirror.

"Les, take them off the counter. There's no room."

The door opened and Jeffrey Penner walked in.

I hadn't spoken to him since our encounter in the nurse's office, but he wasn't someone I'd easily forget. He sashayed awkwardly to the counter, his silly grin plastered on his face.

"Hey Leslie, hi. What are you doing here?"

"This is my father's store. Dad—this is Jeffrey. He's from my school."

"How do you do?" murmured my father, sizing him up.

"Hello, Mr. Marx. Hey Les. How've you been? Long time no see."

"I've been fine. Busy."

"Yeah, I bet. School and all . . . What's that you're holding?"

The dolls went damp in my hands. "Oh. Nothing. Just some old junk I found in the back room."

"Let me see." He took the one in the bride's dress and turned it this way and that. "My sister would love them," he said. "She's ten."

"Why don't you take them?"

"No, I couldn't. They're yours. I mean, I assumed they were . . ."

"It's okay, I don't *play* with them anymore. I just found them in the office desk."

He shoved the doll back to me. "No, you'd better keep them. You might be sentimental about them or something. Anyway, they're too good for Melissa."

My father cleared his throat. "Excuse me for interrupting, but did you come in to buy something? Originally?"

"Oh." Jeff's face turned almost the same color as his hair. "Yeah. I have a list. My dad was fixing a vent in the attic and he ran out . . ." He dug down into his pocket. "There's a bunch of things he wanted."

"Why don't you let me get them," my father said wearily. "It will save time."

"Thanks. I am kind of slow on my feet."

"I meant, I know where things are. Let me see your list." He held it at arm's length to read and then left to collect the items. Jeffrey leaned his elbows on the counter.

"I didn't know your dad owned this place," he said. "I've been here before."

"I'm surprised at you slipping up. You did such a thorough job researching me."

Jeff grinned. "I do great work, don't I? Of course, you're a worthwhile subject."

"Me?"

"Absolutely. You're a Future Famous Person. Probably the only one I'll ever meet. Not to mention that you're a suffering cripple like me." He winced. "Oh, my gosh, I'm sorry," he said. "I forgot you don't like it when I'm flippant."

"And insensitive."

"Oh no, not that, not really. It's a front."

"I see. Underneath, you're gentle, caring . . ."

He interrupted. "I am not a creep," he intoned. "I respect motherhood, love dogs, and allow little old ladies to help me across the street."

My father came back then with an armful of aluminum mesh and a fistful of screws, tacks, and staples. He dumped everything on the counter.

"Good grief," said Jeff. "What's my father building, a house?"

"More like a rabbit hutch," I said.

My father started to ring up the sale. "So, you go to Leslie's school," he said as he worked. "Are you in any classes together? Maybe you like music . . ."

"Oh, no, not me. I'm afraid I have absolutely no talents. But I'm a big fan of Leslie's."

"Jeffrey, how could you possibly be my fan? You've never heard me play. In fact, I'll bet you've never listened to classical music in your life."

"So?" My father shrugged. "He can start. The boy doesn't have to pass an examination just to listen." He packed Jeff's purchases in a bag. "Music is the universal language, right? Everyone should learn to appreciate it."

"Absolutely," said Jeff. "I'm willing to start any time, Les. Whenever you are."

"That'll be $26.46," said my father.

It took Jeff a minute's searching, but he came up with two twenties. My dad rang it up and handed him the change, which Jeff stuffed in his pocket. Then he scooped up his bulky parcel with both hands.

"Do you need some help getting that to your car?" my father asked. "Fred can take it for you."

"Oh no, I'm fine." He edged his chin over the top of the paper bag. The roll of aluminum screen stuck out at an angle beside his head, totally blocking his view to one side.

"Wait, I'll get the door for you," I said.

I held it open and he skated by. Outside, the air was clean and snappy, a perfect autumn day.

"Does that thing actually run?" I asked, as he blundered his way to an ancient green car. "Be careful putting that package in. The weight might be too much for it."

"For this car? The Green Gumdrop? Never. It's indestructible."

"You've named it. How sixties."

"Well, the car is from the sixties. Practically." He hoisted the parcel into the trunk and slammed the lid. "But it's mine, all mine."

"Really?"

"My mother gave her to me. Used to be hers. And you know Volvos, they never die. They just go on and on forever until you're sick of them." He grinned, and patted the hood. "Want to cruise?"

"No, thanks." I paused a moment. "It must be nice, having your own car. Being able to go where you want."

"Oh, it is. It's great. So far, I've been able to drive myself to school and to the hardware store, any time I feel like it." I laughed.

Jeff walked around and opened the driver's door. He draped one arm over it and leaned toward me. "You know," he said, "I believe you're beginning to like me. My boyish charm is winning you over."

"Think so?"

"Definitely. Well, it's hard to resist someone who worships the ground you walk on. Oops. Have I done it again?"

"It's all right. I'm not that sensitive."

He scratched his ear. "Maybe you'd like to, uh, join me for lunch. At school, I mean."

"I practice during lunch."

"I could listen."

"Oh, well, I don't know . . ."

"Les!" It was my father, calling from the store. "Les, what's keeping you?"

"Coming, Daddy. Just talking to Jeff a minute." I turned back.

"I'd like to hear you play," he said. "They say you're very good."

"Well . . ." I thought of the practice room, the forced solitude each day. Maybe I could play with someone listening. I hadn't had lunch with anyone in weeks. "You'd have to get a pass," I said.

"So? No problem." Jeff gave a quick salute and got into the car. "I'll see you Monday," he said. Like it was settled.

I went back inside. My father was behind the counter, tidying things. "He's gone?"

"Yeah."

He raised his eyebrows. "Young man certainly talks enough. Is he always like that?"

"As far as I know. He never stops for breath."

"Well. It's a reaction." He polished the glass counter-top with his sleeve, slow, deliberate circles. "What's the matter with him, exactly?"

"What do you mean? Oh. His legs. Cerebral palsy, I think. Don't you remember? There were some kids with it in the hospital when I . . ."

"I didn't recall." He flicked a speck off the now gleaming glass. "Why don't you take those dolls in back, Leslie. You look ridiculous sitting here with them."

"Oh. The dolls. All right." I placed them gently in the box and closed it. But I couldn't quite bring myself to part with them. When we went home for lunch, I took them with me and squirreled them in the back of my nightstand drawer. They were simply too pretty to throw away.

CHAPTER · 7

DESPITE JEFF'S BRASH ASSURANCE, I didn't actually expect him to show up on Monday. But he did. He was waiting for me by the lockers at lunchtime when I went to get my violin. And when I headed downstairs to the practice room, he trailed me like a puppy. Just as if he'd been invited.

"Aren't you likely to get in trouble for cutting class like this? Or lunch, or whatever?" I asked.

"Don't worry about it, it's all taken care of." He waved a slip of paper like a tiny flag. "I told them I was helping you with your books." And to prove the point, he wrestled the music out of my hand and stumped away cheerfully beside me.

Down in the basement, it was quiet and deserted. The practice room, with its soundproof ceiling, deadened our voices. I flicked on the overhead light and set my violin on a vacant chair. Jeff settled into another.

"Hey, nifty," he said, taking it all in. "Just imagine, privacy in school." He began to unwrap his lunch. "I came prepared," he said. "Made my own sandwich. My mother's cooking is hazardous to your health. Like eating in Mexico." He took a hefty bite. "You eat before or after?" he said, with his mouth full.

"I usually wolf everything in five minutes."

"Well, don't let me cramp your style."

I smiled, and pulled up a chair facing him. They were the kind with little desks attached. I hoped my mother hadn't made me anything smelly, like tuna fish, or salami.

"How long have you been playing the violin?" asked Jeff as he ate.

"Oh, a long time. Since I was seven."

"And were you a genius from the start?"

"Genius? No. But I loved it from the start. It was right after my accident."

"Hmm. Heavy. Gave you something to live for, that kind of thing?"

"I guess so. And my father—he encouraged me, you know? He's always had a thing for music." I peeked inside my sandwich. Good. Swiss cheese. Took a bite.

"I sure wish I had something like that," said Jeff. "Something brilliant, and unique. You know? To set me apart from the crowd."

"Jeffrey, believe me. You don't have to worry about being lost in the shuffle."

"Oh. Well. I guess you're right, at that. I do have a sort of outstanding dorkiness."

"That's not what I meant."

"It's okay, you know. I'm not sensitive about it."

I took a few bites of the rather dry sandwich.

"How about the rest of your family?" asked Jeff. "Everyone else musical, too?"

"No. My father, like I said. But he only listens, he doesn't play. Not anymore, he stopped years ago. And my brother, he's—I think he has talent, but he never cared much for routine. You know. Practicing every day." I brushed off my fingers and took a quick swig of juice. "I'd better start," I said.

"Please do."

I used the little towelette my mother sends to clean my fingers, and then unsnapped my violin case. I have two violins, an excellent older one, and a new, good, but less expensive backup. I only take the backup to school. I took it out, quickly tuned, and ran up and down a scale to loosen up.

"Do you have to keep looking at me?" I said.

"Of course. By the way, that was good."

"That was a *scale*."

I shut my eyes and tried to concentrate on my warm-ups. I usually abbreviate them at lunchtime, so I have time for some music. I limbered up just enough to play. Then, what the hey, I thought. I'll show him what it's really about. I fished out the music for the Bach Chaconne.

It wasn't really practicing, what I did. Practicing is picking apart, working out kinks and trouble spots. What I did was to play right through. I hit a few snags, of course—it's a devilish hard piece—but I plowed on and kept going, for a full quarter of an hour. It's music that

sends chills down my spine, from the first gut-wrenching
double stop to the last quiver of the strings. When I was
done, I looked over at Jeff to see what he thought. I guess
I half-expected him to make some brainless, trendy re-
mark: "Wow," or "Awesome." But he didn't say anything.

Finally I said, "That's my favorite piece."

"I think I can understand that," he said. He paused.
"You should play for people, Leslie."

I shook my head. "You can't play stuff like that. It's
not what audiences expect. They want glitter. You know.
Paganini. Flying fingers."

"Maybe you underestimate them."

"You sound like my teacher." I sniffed. "She's always
hammering at me—to give recitals, to get on stage. Get
experience for my audition."

"What audition? What do you do, anyway, with the
violin? When you grow up."

I started to put away my instrument, buffing it first with
a cloth. "It all depends on how good you are. The next
step, for someone like me, is auditioning for a good
school—Juilliard or Manhattan. Then, after you graduate
. . ." I turned my hand palm-up. "If you're great, you
become a soloist. Like Perlman or Zukerman. If you're
good, you get an orchestra job."

"How about if you're okay?"

"You fall off the edge of the world."

"What?"

I laughed. "If you're just okay, you don't get into a
school like Juilliard in the first place. That's one reason
it's such a big deal."

"And you don't think you'll get in?"

"I didn't say that. But . . ." I hesitated. "Look. I know I'm good. I just don't like playing in front of people. Showing off like a trained seal."

"Didn't you like playing for me?"

"That was different." I picked up the violin case and hugged it to my chest. "This didn't feel like a performance. It felt like . . ."

"Playing for a friend," he finished for me. I nodded. "Thank you," he said. "I guess I could enjoy thinking of myself as your friend."

We gathered our belongings and stepped out into the hall. I started to speak, hesitated, then pushed myself on. "Jeff. I wonder if I could ask you for something. A favor."

"A favor? Absolutely." He bowed. "Anything at all. The moon on a plate."

"It's not that dramatic. I was just wondering if . . . well, you remember the other day, when we were talking about your car. And I said . . ."

"You wished you had one. So you could go places."

"Yeah. Well, I'd like to go someplace. To see my brother. I was wondering if you could take me."

"Where is he?"

"Oh, it's not far, just up in North Jersey. He's in college . . ." I stopped myself. "He's living up there."

He deliberated a moment. "I think I could manage that. When?"

"Saturday?"

"That should be fine."

And so that Saturday at ten I walked down the block and found Jeff and the Gumdrop waiting for me. It was a gray, overcast morning, but Jeff was full of good humor. He grinned when he saw me coming, and reached across

to swing open the door. It was obvious he had taken some
pains with his appearance. His face was pink, his clothes
spruced up for the occasion. He couldn't do much with
his hair. He'd plastered it down with water, but it was
already springing out in corkscrews where it was starting
to dry.

"Come into my parlor," he said. "How do you like it?
I even vacuumed in your honor."

"Really? I'm glad you told me." I sat on the edge of
the seat and carefully swung my legs around. "Jeffrey,
this car's not going to die on us, is it?"

"Die? Oh no, she's very reliable. But, Les—why all the
secrecy? Why'd you have me park down the street?"

"I didn't want my parents to know. I told them I was
going to the library with Bobbie."

"Why? Is it some kind of crime for you to visit your
brother?"

"It's a long story." And as Jeff started the car and
headed us north, I sketched it for him, the whole painful
history. Steve. My father. Steve's quitting school. And
me, caught in the middle, feeling guilty, no matter what
I did.

"What I'm not sure about," said Jeff when I finished,
"is what you expect to accomplish by seeing him. It
sounds like his mind is made up. Or do you just miss
him?"

"Of course I miss him," I said irritably. "I haven't set
eyes on him since September. And even on the phone
he's been . . . I don't know. Evasive. He won't say anything about himself with my mother and father on the
line." I gazed out the window into the gloom. What *did*
I hope to gain, seeing him? Then I remembered how it

was when Steve lived at home. How I used to visit him in his room when he was in trouble. I'd wait till my father's anger cooled, maybe till he was out of the house, and then I'd slip into Steve's room and just hang out. The two of us together, doing puzzles or reading—comics, usually, in his case. Sometimes I'd smuggle him a Nestlé's bar in my sleeve or violin case. I'd even brought one today. I had it right beside me, tucked in a paper bag.

By the time we got to Steve's block, the first drops of rain were starting to fall. There was no parking anywhere; Jeff circled the block twice before pulling up at the curb.

"He is expecting you, I hope?" Jeff asked. "You told him you were coming, didn't you?"

"Yeah, he knows."

"Why don't I drop you off, then. You'd probably like some time alone. I'll look around for parking, and when I find a spot I'll come up."

"Well . . . thanks. You know the apartment number? 3D?"

"3D. I love it. Like a Vincent Price horror movie. Don't worry, I'll find you. See you in a few minutes."

So I entered the dingy vestibule and took the elevator to the third floor.

CHAPTER · 8

I REALLY WASN'T PREPARED for my joy at seeing my brother. I hadn't realized I missed him so much. I rang the bell and he answered right away, swinging the door wide. Strange, I thought, he looks the same. But, of course, it had only been a few weeks. He was paler, that was all, the summer color almost gone. His sandy, wavy hair needed a cut. But to me he was beautiful, just the sight of him.

He stepped aside and ushered me in. And my God, what a mess! How could he stand it? My mother's cleanliness sometimes gets on my nerves, too, but I never considered going quite so far to the opposite extreme. I stepped gingerly over the kitty kibble that was spilled on the floor and looked past the filthy kitchen table to a living room littered with books and tape cassettes and cast-off clothes.

"Have a seat?" Steve motioned to a stained, rumpled sofa. "I know it looks grungy, but we don't have bed-bugs."

I lowered myself cautiously. Steve sat opposite in one of those squishy foam chairs that fold into beds. It was so soft he nearly disappeared, except for the long legs sprawled in front of him. From some crevice in the book-shelf he unearthed a pack of gum, took out a stick, and offered me one. I shook my head.

"Still passing up the sweets?" he said, putting it away.

"Gum hardly counts."

"No, I . . . It gives me a stomachache, that's all." He caught me gazing about at the room, and I quickly offered an excuse. "I didn't remember your place too well," I said. "I only came the once, you know. With Mom and Dad, when you moved in."

"Well, it's a little messy this morning. We had a party last night."

"Oh?" I tried to sound casual.

"No big deal," Steve went on. "A few friends, girl-friends. A bottle of wine."

"I get the picture."

Steve stretched like a cat and scratched his belly. "Well, never mind about me," he said. "How's my bril-liant baby sister coming along? Hard at work, with your books and music and all? You get booked into Carnegie Hall yet?"

"No. Don't tease, Steve, all right?"

"I'm just trying to make pleasant conversation. I mean, I was surprised when you called, I thought maybe you had big news or something. By the way, who brought you? You get a lift with Bobbie?"

"Uh, Bobbie and I have had a . . . disagreement. We're not seeing much of one another these days."

"No, really? You had a fight? I didn't know Bobbie had it in her."

"Well, it seems I offended her. Something about her boyfriend."

"Ah." He nodded. "Always a delicate subject. So, who drove you, then?"

"Another friend. You don't know him, his name's Jeff."

"*Your* boyfriend?"

"Nothing like that." As I shook my head, I noticed the wicked glint in his hazel eyes. "Don't get any wrong ideas," I said.

"What's wrong with them?"

"*Steve.*" He snorted. "Anyway, I didn't come to talk about me. It's you I want to talk about. You sounded so . . . distracted on the phone the other day. You're worrying me."

"Why? I'm fine, Les. Having a wonderful time."

"That's what I'm afraid of."

"Oh, Leslie, don't go all moral on me. What are you upset about? Maybe—horrors!—you think I'm on drugs?"

"Are you?"

"Only slightly. You know, when we have a party, or we're just hanging around . . ."

"All right, Steven, all right. But that's not the main thing. What's really worrying me is, what you're doing with yourself all day. I know you're not going to classes, and I don't think you're working."

"It's called constructive nothingness. It's a high art."

"And you're pursuing it on Dad's money."

"Who are you, his accountant?" Steve tossed his head briskly. "Les, I don't know what's gotten into you lately. You're so conservative. You're as bad as they are."

"*They?* Mom and Dad, you mean?"

"Yes, *they*. The enemy."

I crossed my arms in front of me. What a juvenile attitude—just like him: the enemy. "Steve, no one wants to hurt you," I said gently. "Not Mom and Dad, certainly not me. I just don't like to see you throwing your life away, that's all. Hanging around the apartment doing nothing. Like you've given up."

"Why shouldn't I? Everyone else gave up on me years ago."

"That's not true." For a moment we sat silent. "Oh," I said. "I almost forgot. I brought you something." I held out my paper bag.

"What is it, a rock?"

"No. This one's from me to you."

He peered inside. "A Nestlé's Crunch," he said. "My favorite."

"Oh, good, I got it right. You still like them."

"Of course. And . . . thanks for the memory."

Abruptly, he rose and tossed the bag on the chair. He walked to the window and looked out at the gloom. "I can see you remember the old days. All those visits you made when I was in Siberia." Sharply, he turned to face me. "Leslie. I don't want your chocolate. I don't want any more presents from you."

I was too puzzled even to frame a question. I stared at him. Hadn't he just told me he liked it?

"I can get my own chocolate," he said. "I don't want it smuggled in while I'm locked in my room."

"I don't have the faintest idea what you're talking about."

"Sure you do, Les. Isn't that why you came? To sweeten it up for me, make it bearable? To persuade me it wouldn't be so bad, being in prison?"

"What prison?"

"School. College. Victor's plans. What else?"

I leaned back in my seat and rubbed my forehead. "All right," I said. "I confess. I'm completely mystified. Steve, I didn't come on Daddy's say-so."

"Then stop trying to fix things up. They're past fixing. I've quit and that's the end of it."

"Well, why don't you tell him, then? Why can't you at least be honest about it?"

"Why? Because I'm not the sweetheart. Okay? Because I'm Daddy's bad boy." The color flared in his cheeks. "Les, don't you realize Victor has been waiting years for this opportunity? The chance to throw me out in good conscience? I'm making him happy. I've finally screwed up on a grand scale, so he can wash his hands of me and feel good about it. And if I lie a little, mooch a little, take him for a short ride—well, that's all right, he owes me. He owes me for twenty years of . . ." His voice trailed off. "Child abuse," he muttered.

I stared at him. Talk about laying it on thick. "I'm beginning to think Daddy's right," I said. "You really do want to fail. What are you going to do with yourself, may I ask? After he finds out, that is, and gives you the boot?"

"After I leave this lap of luxury, you mean? Jesus, Leslie, I don't know. I'll get a job."

"What kind of job? What skills do you have? You won't have finished college."

"Not everyone goes to college. I'll get a job. I'll be a shoe salesman, a hot dog vendor. You think everyone goes to the *Juilliard* School?"

Well, I thought. Now the cards are on the table.

"Steven, don't blame me," I said. "This is your problem, not mine. I was only—"

"Wait, don't tell me. Trying to help." His eyes narrowed. "A regular angel of mercy."

"Don't."

"What's the matter, did I hit a nerve? Come on, Les, be honest for once. Isn't it fun, just a little? Watching me catch it time after time? As long as you know it'll never be your turn."

"Never my . . . For God's sake, Steven, why should it be my turn?" My voice came out high and wobbly. "You practically ask for it. Why don't you ever think first? I know you're smart, Steve, I know you're capable. You understand Dad as well as I do. Why do you always have to do stuff that gets on his nerves? Why do you . . ."

"What? Eat candy? Or read Marvel comics? Why do I like pretty girls with nice round tits? I enjoy life, Leslie. That makes it hard for me to give it up."

"No one's asking you to do that."

"Aren't you? I think that's just what you're asking. But you see, Les, it's very hard for me. I'm not the same as you, I'm not a saint. I have these inconvenient feelings, these human urges. I like pleasure. You know what that is, pleasure? No, maybe you don't, at that."

He pushed himself away from the window and went back to his seat, slumped deep in the cushions and stretching his long legs. "You just can't accept it, can you?" He passed his hands over his face. "That nothing will work for me. That, no matter how hard I try, no matter what I choose, it will be wrong, because I'm the one choosing it. You think it's just a question of sticking to the rules. That if I humored him a little he'd love me, just the way he loves you."

"He does love you, Steven. But you disappoint him. Over and over again. With these silly things you do."

"Oh, Les," he murmured. "It's so sad, it's funny. How clever you think you are. Tell me, was it something you did that gave you talent? That made you love to practice violin, instead of messing with a car? Leslie—you're golden—perfect. In your whole life, you've never felt one moment's disapproval. But you don't want to admit that it was just luck."

I sat very still. My hands dropped to my lap and I saw my legs, the baggy pants I was wearing to cover them. An odd stretch of the word, to call me perfect.

"It's very neat," I said at last. "A very neat excuse."

There was a buzz at the door. And then, dimly, I recollected: Jeff. Steve went to answer and I followed a step behind.

"Good grief, Les. You sure picked a wonderful day for an outing." Jeff stood dripping in the hallway. His hair was slick with rain and he toweled himself with his sleeve.

"Hi, I'm Jeff Penner." He and Steve shook hands. "I'm sorry to interrupt. I knew you'd want to talk, but it got so stuffy in the car."

"That's all right. I think we're finished," said Steve, looking at Jeff as he spoke. "I think we've beaten the subject to the ground."

Finished, I thought. What a word. How can you finish a brother?

"What do you want me to say to Daddy?" I asked. "I mean, if the subject comes up. You want me to say I was here?"

"Say whatever you want to, Leslie. It doesn't matter."

"You know I'm not good at secrets." I added, softer, "He'll cut your money, Steve. The minute he finds out."

"So be it."

I turned to Jeff. "Well, then, I guess I'm ready. To go, I mean."

"Go? I just got here." He looked back and forth from Steve to me. "All right, you're the boss." He shrugged and gave Steve a lopsided grin. "It was good meeting you, anyway."

"Yeah. A pleasure." The door shut behind us, echoing in the gray hall.

CHAPTER · 9

JEFF AND I TOOK the elevator to the first floor and stepped out to the street. It was raining in earnest, the drops so dark and heavy you expected them to stain your clothing.

"The car's about three blocks," he said. "Do you want me to come back for you?"

I shook my head. "No, I'll walk. It's . . . I like the cold. Steve's room—I was sweating in there." And we slogged off through the puddles.

It was stupid, of course. Exhausting, too far. I was drenched to the skin. In the car, our breath instantly fogged the windows. My back collar was soaked and the water collected and ran down my neck. I stared at the windshield, but the glass was too cloudy to see out. Beside me, Jeff sat for once quiet and still.

"Do you want to talk?" he said at last. I shook my head. "I'd be happy to listen."

"No." I searched my bag for a tissue. The tears were already spilling. "Let's just . . . let's just go."

He started the engine and pulled out into the busy street. The rain hammered on the roof; sheets of water blurred the window glass. The car smelled of wet clothes and musty upholstery and exhaust fumes mixed together. A confusion. Everything a confusion. All my life I'd loved Steve and thought that he loved me. How could I have misunderstood so much?

I must have been lost in my thoughts a long time. When I looked up, we were already off the main road and nearing home. Jeff turned down an unfamiliar street.

"Where are we going?"

"My house. I think if you go home looking like that, your mother might suspect you weren't at the library."

He drove me down tree-lined streets into an older neighborhood. The houses were big, comfortable. Set far back from the road. The car crunched over a gravel driveway and came to a stop in front of a large white house. It was messy—run-down, even. But I liked the big maples out front, the tall columns flanking the front steps.

Jeff came around to my side to open the door. "I think we have the place to ourselves."

"Are you sure that's all right?" What would my mother say, I wondered. I couldn't decide which would bother her more, my imposing on the Penners, or my being with Jeff alone.

"Oh, someone'll be back soon. They're at the store or something." He held out a hand and I carefully swung my feet onto the gravel drive. "Come on in and see the rest of the place," he said cheerfully. "Don't let the classy appearance fool you. Really it's a wreck. Everything's broken—the plumbing, the roof—that's the only reason we could afford it. My dad spends every spare minute fixing it up."

He unlocked the front door and we stepped into a narrow hall. There was a damp mildew smell, probably from the dust-colored carpet. But you could see it had once been lovely. There were French doors in the living room, opening onto a flagstone patio, and a broad white mantel with an antique clock on top. The furniture was a mix of new and old, nice and ratty—antique clocks and moth-eaten rugs. Papers and books were piled on every surface. But, in spite of the clutter, there was a soothing quiet here, in the high ceilings and cool plaster walls.

"You want some food?" called Jeff from the kitchen. "I can offer you clam dip, old cheese, and bologna—no, forget that."

"Maybe just a drink. Something hot?"

He glanced over. "Come to think of it, you do look chilled." He put on a kettle and went off to adjust the thermostat. In a couple of minutes, the steam came on with a moan and a shudder. Jeff dug out some potato chips and dip and helped me to a seat. "I'd really like to roll out the red carpet for you," he said, "but it's got moth holes. Like everything else in this place." He poured me a mug of tea.

"No, don't apologize. I like your house. It's gracious. Comfortable."

"That's a polite way of putting it. And I guess it'll be nice someday, by the time I'm in college. For now it makes my mom happy. She fell in love with the lot, 'all the garden possibilities.' She's a landscape designer. Would you like some cookies? No? Maybe you'd like to see the outside. Or else I could show you my room. If you don't think that's improper on a first date."

"No, it's fine. Anything you want to do."

I followed Jeff upstairs. He was so gawky, as he climbed. Pigeon-toed, all elbows and knees. But full of energy. Walking didn't tire him, as it did me. He led me to his door and flicked on the light. He was smiling and almost trembling with eagerness. I could actually see the pounding of his chest through his thin cotton shirt.

"God, I can't believe you're here," he rattled on. "Do you know how long I've been dreaming of this? Jeez. Come in, Les, sit down." He gave me a gentle nudge into a big upholstered chair and began prowling the room, pulling stuff off the shelves. "I mean, we've been friends at school, but I never thought . . . I never really believed . . . Oh, I've got so much to show you. Where do I start? But promise you'll stop me if I get boring. I mean, don't be polite, 'cause I know I get carried away, that's one of my faults. Here, look at this. Do you like cars? Probably not. But this one's kind of nice, it's a '62 Corvette, a Matchbox car, see? I have hundreds of them, mint condition. I used to be really into this stuff. And see this one? It's an antique, a Duesenberg. Isn't that cute?"

"Yes." I'd never actually looked at a Matchbox car before. I examined the tiny headlights, the steering wheel. Everything where it should be.

"I was nuts about these for a while. And then I—Say, do you want to listen to some music? I've got a stereo. Although I probably haven't got anything you'd like."

"The quiet is fine."

"No. Come on, you just don't want to hurt my feelings. Here." He flicked on the radio and twiddled the knob up and down, filling the room with a jumble of noise. "What station do you like? You'd better decide, I don't know what to do with this thing."

I leaned forward. It took me a moment to remember the frequency of WNYC, although I listen to it every day. Unfortunately, they were playing some overblown orchestral piece—Bruckner, maybe. I left it.

"Isn't that wonderful," said Jeff. "You see? Why don't I listen to stuff like that? 'Because you're an idiot, Jeffrey.' God, Les, I really am glad you're here. I mean—I know you're upset and not at your best, but—hey, maybe I can cheer you up."

"Thank you. And you are, Jeff. I'm feeling much better already."

"You ever read this?" he said, from the far side of the room. "Ursula Le Guin? I was really into science fiction and fantasy for a while. I read all her stuff. Tolkien, too. Do you like him? And then—"

"Jeffrey," I said.

"What? I'm boring you, right? 'Cause I explained, you can just tell me to shut up, whenever . . ."

"No, you're not boring me. In fact—oh, I've got to turn this music off, it's horrible." I clicked the knob and the silence came down like a blanket. "That's better." I looked around slowly, trying to take everything in. "I like your things," I said. "The cars, and books. You said you couldn't do anything. But you do much more than me."

"I can't do anything *well*. I pick up a hobby for a while, then I switch to something else. I don't have any perseverance, that's my problem."

"Maybe what you've got is better. You have"—I leaned back lightly in the big chair—"spontaneity."

"Sounds like a nice word for shallow."

"I didn't mean it that way. It's like Steve, you know? My brother. He always had lots of hobbies—" I stopped short.

"Hey," said Jeff, coming closer. He reached out lightly and brushed the hair from my cheek. "Don't get depressed about it, huh? Whatever it was." I shook my head. For a moment he stayed close beside me but then turned and sat on the bed opposite. His feet dangled pigeon-toed; his light-blue eyes never left me.

"I don't know where to start," I said.

"Start with you. I don't care about him."

"I don't know why I do, so much. But I can't seem to help it." I swallowed. "Jeff—what makes a person quit on himself like that? Just give up trying and sit back—take whatever comes."

"Is that what Steve's doing?"

I raised a hand. "As far as I can tell, he's hanging around the apartment chewing gum. Or worse. It's like he's lost faith in the idea of accomplishing. Doesn't believe in it anymore."

"Maybe he doesn't know what he wants yet. Hasn't figured it out."

"You think so?" I looked up hopefully. "You think maybe he just needs time? To collect his thoughts and figure himself out?"

"Could be. I gather you never had to do that, but lots of people do."

I nodded slowly. "You're right about me, I suppose. I knew the first time I picked up the violin. The first time I stroked the bow and felt the sound go through me. You know, the vibration. It was like a current, electricity. Going right through my bones."

He stared at me intently. I touched my face; it was warm. I get like that sometimes, talking about the violin. I let my hands fall to my lap.

"Do you know what you want to do?" I said slowly, steering the conversation toward safer ground.

"When I grow up, you mean?" I nodded. "No. I haven't thought that far ahead. But I could think of what I'd like to do now."

The room was very quiet. Only at the window was there sound, the steady drip of rain falling from the gutter to the earth below.

"Les," he said. He leaned toward me. I could see the white skin of his neck where his collar opened.

"No," I whispered.

"Les. You're so pretty. When you were talking about your music, your face . . ."

From below came the heavy crunching of car wheels on gravel, and the abrupt silence of an engine being cut.

"It's my mother," said Jeff. "With her flawless sense of timing." He ran his hands through his hair. "We can go down if you want, maybe Lyssa's with her. You can meet them both." He sounded reluctant, but relief washed over me.

"Oh. Great." I got up and followed Jeff down the stairs, reaching the bottom just as Jeff's mother came in. "Hi, sweets," she said to Jeff, and then saw me. "Well, hello," she added. "Hello and how do you do."

"Mom, this is Leslie Marx," said Jeff. "A charming and fantastically talented girl from my school. Who for some reason decided I was worth a visit."

"Hi, I'm pleased to meet you. I'm Daphne Penner."

She stretched out her hand. It was rough, and the nails were short and dirt-stained. Her light-brown hair was tied back in a ponytail, and she wore a flannel shirt and slim jeans. She seemed very young for a mother.

For a moment we stood awkwardly in the hall. Then she smiled. "You kids been making yourself at home?"

"Yeah. I was showing Leslie my junk. Can you believe it? Here she is, this brilliant musician and much too good for me, but she actually sat and listened to me babble."

"What kind of musician are you?" she asked.

"Violinist."

"Isn't that a difficult instrument?"

"Well . . ." I started.

"You should hear her," interrupted Jeff. "Honestly, it's impressive."

Mrs. Penner laughed. "Jeff, that's enough. You're embarrassing everyone. Leslie, would you like a bite of food? I'm sure my son didn't offer you."

"Oh no, he did. But no, thanks, I have to go. Jeff was just about to drive me." I looked pointedly at him.

"So soon? Well, we'll meet again, I'm sure. Jeff, you be careful, all right? The roads are slick."

"Yes, Mother. Come on, Les."

We walked together to the now-muddy Gumdrop. Jeff opened the door and helped me in. Now that we were alone, we were awkward again; Jeff spent ages settling in his seat.

"I'm sorry," he said. "Upstairs, if I . . . I didn't mean to come on strong. It was the wrong moment." He clumsily patted my hand. "Don't worry about Steve. He'll be okay. He's adjusting."

"I hope so. You didn't get to see it, but he's so sweet,

really. When he's not upset. And smart, too. Clever. Good with his hands. If only . . ." I looked up at Jeff. "Do you think I should tell them? My parents, I mean?"

"Is that your responsibility?"

I didn't know the answer to that one. Steve had felt like my responsibility for a long time. "Well, I don't suppose I can," I said. "If it comes to that."

"Then don't." He flashed me a dazzling smile. "Leslie. If you'd lavish that devotion on me, I'd be your slave for life."

He started the car and we headed for home. I wasn't sure that devotion was the right word for what he wanted—at least, not the sisterly type. But, whatever you called it, I didn't seem to have it to give. Why not, though? What was wrong with the idea? I remembered him leaning toward me, his lips open in a smile. His white skin peeking through his collar. My hands dropped to my lap and I rested my forehead on the window, feeling the cold glass and the sharp jolting of the car on the bumpy road.

CHAPTER · 10

As it turned out, Jeff's consideration in taking me to his house was unnecessary. My house was empty. My father still at work, my mother shopping, probably. Her weekly chores. I went to the kitchen and found myself some odds and ends to eat—bread and butter, cheese. When I was done, I put the dishes in the sink and sat awhile at the table. The room was dim in this cloudy weather. The light bulbs burning overhead looked stark and lonely.

Steve and I had never had such harsh words before. Of course we'd fought, as kids do. Squabbling. Over games, or which show to watch on TV. But even when we fought, we were somehow allied. The children: a unit. Now that was split open. What had he called me? Perfect?

A saint? Of all the absurd labels. And then, suddenly, I remembered my talk with Bobbie a few weeks back. What was it she said? Something jogged my memory. Or maybe it was her tone of voice, or mine. I thought I'd been trying to help her, I now recalled. Trying to save her from a mistake.

I went back to the hallway and put on my coat. Outside, on the porch, the wind gusted, but at least the rain had stopped. I pulled my collar tight as I walked to Bobbie's house. It took some resolution to ring the bell.

"Who is it?" came a voice. And then, closer, "Yeah?" She opened and saw me. "Oh." A moment's silence. "Les. Hi."

There was a lot of noise behind her. Her brothers, screaming. The TV. "Hi," I echoed. "I . . . I came to see how you're doing. If you were still all right."

"I'm fine." She shut the door partway behind her. "Did you want something?"

"No. Just to talk."

One of her brothers came up and stuck his head around her. "I thought it was Paul," he said. "He's supposed to be coming."

"Well, it's not," Bobbie answered, pushing him back. "Go inside, Guy, you're letting the cold in the house. Wait a minute," she said to me. "It's too noisy here, I'll come out where you are."

A moment later she reappeared in a parka. She slammed the door. "Is it too cold for you outside?" she asked.

"No. Not bad. For a while at least."

"You want to sit?"

"Thanks." We settled ourselves into a couple of plastic

deck chairs. I hadn't thought this far; I didn't know how to proceed. "Bobbie . . ."

"Les . . ." We spoke simultaneously. "You first," she said. I swallowed.

"Bobbie. About that talk we had. That argument. Tell me—are you still mad?"

"I don't know. I guess. What made you decide to come over, anyway? To suddenly decide to talk. Did something happen?"

"In a way. Something that made me . . . Bobbie, I want to apologize for what I said. Okay? I never meant to hurt your feelings, or cause some big breakup." I took a long, deep breath, hiking my shoulders. "I just thought I was being a friend." She nodded, not looking me in the eye. I went on. "I visited Steve today, at his apartment. We had a long talk, the two of us. And I began to realize I wasn't acting, coming across, the way I meant to. The way I really feel."

"How's that?"

"Well . . . when I love people—like you, and Steve— I sometimes act, oh . . ."

"High and mighty? Yes, I know." She paused. "I guess I am still angry with you."

"I don't even remember what I said."

"No? I do. You said I was lowering myself. You made me sound like some kind of cheap—well, I don't even want to say it. When all I was really doing was going out with a guy. Someone you thought you didn't like."

"But, Bobbie. You sounded so mixed-up. You weren't even sure *you* liked him, remember? I didn't mean it as a put-down. Maybe it came out sounding that way, but

I said those things because, well, because I think so much of you. Just like Steve and his school. Because I know how wonderful you are, both of you, and—"

"And you think you have the right to decide for us. What's best."

"No! Oh. I don't know." I shook my head. "I just thought you deserved the best. That you shouldn't have to compromise. Because you're wonderful, Bobbie, and . . ."

"Leslie." She held up a hand. "Leslie, I appreciate why you're saying this. But you're wrong. Take a good look at me. I'm not wonderful, I'm ordinary. Very ordinary. And what you said about Eric was right, too. He isn't gorgeous, or captain of the football team. But we're okay for each other. Not everyone is exceptional. Not everyone's like you."

"Like me? Bobbie: now you're doing it. I'm not the only one making judgments."

"What do you mean?"

"It's how everyone thinks about me. You all write me off. Like I have no feelings where boys are concerned. Like I'm simply out of it."

There was a long silence. "But, Les," she said at last. "You said it yourself, a million times. 'I don't have time for dating. I can't be bothered with that stuff.' "

"Well, you shouldn't have believed me!" I shouted. Bobbie covered her face with her hand. When she lifted it, she was smiling.

"You really are an idiot, you know that?" she said.

"I'm discovering it." I shook my head. "But it's true, Bobbie. Why couldn't you guess how much it hurt? Like at lunchtime. Listening to you all talk—you and Celeste—and all of you. Worrying about your little microscopic zits, when I . . . I . . ."

"Oh, Les." She leaned over and threw her arm around me. A big sheepdog embrace. "Why didn't you ever say anything? Why didn't you tell me how you felt all this time?"

"I thought it was obvious. Or should be."

"I figured you wanted to practice. You're always thinking about music. And you *are* talented, you're unique. Why should I expect you to act like the rest of us?"

Because I'm human, I wanted to say. I looked up at her face through a blur of tears. "I . . . there's this boy that likes me," I said softly. "He drove me to Steve's place. Jeff Penner, his name is. You know him?"

"I've seen you together. He seems nice. I'm glad."

I smiled at her. I was overwhelmed with a silly, almost unbearable gratitude. "I need to go," I said. "I have to get home, I haven't practiced yet."

"I'll walk you."

She held my elbow down the slippery steps, and we walked side by side through the puddles.

"You and Jeff go out yet?" she asked. "On a date?"

"No, he hasn't asked me."

"He will." Yes, I thought. She was right. He would have asked already, if he was more formal and proper. "Don't worry," she said, smiling. "You won't die from it. It's actually enjoyable."

"If you say so."

We reached my house and I fumbled in my bag for the key.

"By the way," said Bobbie, "how was Steve, when you found him? He doing all right up there?"

"He's not starving. I guess he's all right."

"You don't sound pleased."

"I'm not. I don't like it at all, what he's doing. It's dishonest. And it's bad for him and bad for the family." I looked up. "Bobbie. Just because you love someone doesn't mean you like everything they do."

She considered a moment. "Fair enough," she said. "But you understand, that goes for me, too. Okay?" I nodded, and she squeezed my arm. "I'm glad you came by, Les. I'll see you Monday. All right?"

"Right."

I found, when I stepped inside, that my mother had returned.

"Oh, you're back," she called from the kitchen. "Did you get some work done? Where are your books?"

I'd almost forgotten my fib about the library.

"I got home a while ago," I said. "Then I went back to Bobbie's. We were talking."

"That's nice. You finished your work, I guess."

How I hated lying to her. I walked in the kitchen and watched her for a moment. She was making pea soup, dropping diced carrots and celery in a big pot. A cloud of steam almost concealed her hands.

"Mom, I have a confession to make."

"What?"

"I didn't go with Bobbie to the library."

She looked at me sharply. "What, then?"

"I was with another friend. A boy. His name's Jeff."

"Oh." She seemed to consider. "He drove you?" I nodded. "Is he a good driver? Responsible?"

"Oh. Very."

"And a nice boy, Les? Not one of those . . ."

"Oh, you'd like him, Mom. I'll bring him next time and you can see for yourself."

"I'd like that. I'd appreciate it very much."

I continued on through the kitchen to my room. So, I thought. So easily deceptions are made.

CHAPTER · 11

Two weeks later, Thanksgiving morning, I woke to the smell of sweet potatoes and chestnuts. I rolled over in bed and stared at the clock. 10 a.m. Ten in the morning, and already my mother was cooking.

Perhaps because we don't celebrate Christmas, Thanksgiving has always been a big holiday at our house. My mother saves all her best recipes, working in each person's favorites, until there is twice as much food as we need. This year, as usual, she'd started early, scouring the papers for good buys. An enormous turkey had been defrosting in the fridge since Tuesday, sharing space with dozens of mysterious bottles, jars, and bowls. "I want to make sure to have enough," she kept saying. "Besides, Steve can use the leftovers."

The smell, though an odd one for morning, was enticing. I hoisted myself around in bed and buckled my straps, then threw on a bathrobe and climbed the stairs to the kitchen.

"Good morning," said my mother brightly. I rubbed my eyes.

"How can you stand that before breakfast?" I said, watching her delve in the raw turkey and bring out some nauseating object. "That thing is sickening."

"It's not before breakfast for me. I've been up since six. Anyway, I want to get started, there's lots to do. Hand me the paprika, would you?"

I went to the closet and got the paprika; also the box of Cheerios. "Where's Daddy?"

"He's in the living room reading the paper. You know how he is, can't survive a day without *The New York Times*." She patted the turkey dry and sprinkled the spice. I opened the fridge to get the milk.

"For goodness' sakes, Mother, are you planning to feed the Russian army?"

"It's not so much. Just turkey and stuffing."

"And sweet potatoes and cranberry mold and—I can hardly find the milk."

"It's on the top shelf, to the right. I don't know what you're complaining about, Leslie, I'm making your favorite things. Where's your holiday spirit?"

I shuddered. Almost said: I left it at Steve's.

After some maneuvering, I found the milk jug and doused my cereal. I started to eat.

"What do you plan to do today?" she asked, eyeing me as she worked. "Dinner's not till four o'clock."

"I hadn't made any plans."

"You going to see Jeffrey?"

"I can't, he's out of town, at his grandmother's. Bobbie's away, too. Don't suppose you need any help?" I added hopefully.

"No, thanks, sweetheart, I've got everything under control." I sighed.

After breakfast, I went back to my room to dress. Then, lacking anything better to do, I drifted out to the living room. My father was sitting in his armchair, engrossed in the newspaper, the headphones strapped to his ears.

"What's on?" I asked, gesturing toward him.

"Hmm?" He saw me and removed the headphones.

"What are you listening to?"

"This? Oh. Beethoven, you want to listen?" He leaned forward and pulled on the cord of the headphones. The jack popped loose and music flooded the room. "One of the Razumovsky quartets," he said, speaking forcefully to be heard over the sound. "It's a beautiful performance."

"Yes. It sounds like it." I sat primly on the sofa nearby.

"Too bad you don't play chamber music," said my father. "It would be pleasant, a group meeting in the house."

I nodded. "What time is Steve coming?" I had to speak loudly to be heard.

"You're asking me? Talk to your mother, that's her department."

I decided to let the matter drop. Since my meeting with Steven a couple of weeks before, communications from him had been thin. He called, though rarely, or waited for my mother to phone him. The conversations themselves tended to the monosyllabic. He was fine. Everything was okay. My guess was that he didn't trust himself to lie and so said nothing. But the talk was so obviously evasive, I wondered that my parents didn't suspect something was wrong. Or maybe they did. With my father it was hard to tell, his distrust was already so great. As for my mother—well, making allowances was her specialty. My mother would never guess at something wrong; she would wait until proof was absolute.

I passed the remainder of the morning practicing, first my usual warm-ups and then a short stint on my Brahms sonata. But for the most part I concentrated on the Mendelssohn. The concerto was my big piece for the audition, and it needed work. By the end of my session, it was just past one. I returned upstairs and found my mother still puttering in the kitchen.

"Gee, I wonder where Steve could be?" My voice was phonily casual.

"I don't know." She checked her watch. "I thought he'd be here by this time. He's probably stuck in traffic. Are you getting hungry? You want some lunch?"

"I don't want to ruin my appetite."

"You won't. Dinner's not for hours yet. Go on into the living room, I'll bring a snack for you and Daddy."

My father was still in his chair. The only change was in the stack of newspaper, rumpled now, resting on the table near his elbow. My mother brought a tray of crackers and cheese.

"I thought you might like a bite," she said, setting it down. "This'll help you wait. Les, would you like a Coke?"

"No," interrupted my father. "I'll get her a drop of sherry. It's a holiday." He disengaged himself from his chair and walked a few steps to the breakfront. "Here, enjoy," he said, holding out an inch in a wineglass. He poured a short one for himself. *"L'chaim."*

It wasn't that I'd never had wine before. Just not very often. I swirled the thick amber liquid and took a cautious sip. Sweet and warm. The tingle started on my tongue and ended at my fingertips.

"So what time did our son say he was coming? Since we're all awaiting his pleasure?" Now it was my father's turn to ask. But before my mother could repeat her stock reply, he went on. "Why don't you call him?" he said. "See if he's even left yet. Or if he's planning to hold us up all night."

"All right." She pushed the plate of hors d'oeuvres in my direction. "Eat something, Leslie. With that wine, on an empty stomach, you'll be sick before you know it."

A strange sinking was coming over me. I took a cracker and chewed it conscientiously, but it refused to dissolve in my mouth. The edges were sharp and hurt my palate. My mother went off to the kitchen to phone and my father sat back in his chair and shut his eyes. Suddenly I was certain that Steve wasn't coming. It was late already. He lived only an hour away. And it added up too well, what I knew and they, my parents, didn't. Steve was such a clumsy liar; my father always caught him out. He knew that if he came, the whole story, his dropping out and concealing it, everything, would be in the open. He couldn't face it. At the last minute, he'd chickened out, the way he always did. I thought of all those sweet potatoes my mother had mashed, all that turkey no one would eat. How could Steve have told her to expect him?

Slowly I got up and followed my mother to the kitchen. She had the phone to her ear. With every ring, she gave the slightest shake of the head.

"No answer?" I asked, as she hung up.

"I let it ring ten times. He's on his way, then."

And there was something so hopeful in her tone that I couldn't bear it. "Mom—did he definitely say yes, that he was coming?"

"Of course he did. How could he not come Thanksgiving Day? It's unthinkable . . ." She broke off and gave me a narrow look. "Leslie, what's up?" she said. "You know something. Tell me."

I never meant to tell. I looked around at the clutter, all the fixings, her hard work. "Nothing," I mumbled.

"What? Tell me, Les. What is it?"

"I . . ." I stopped. She came close and held my chin and turned my face toward her, so I could not escape her soft, anxious glance.

"Steve's dropped out of school," I whispered. "That's why he's been avoiding you. He was afraid to tell Dad."

"What?"

I pulled back, but she followed me, brushing back my hair with her hand.

"You knew? You knew about his quitting?" She lowered her voice. "How long ago . . ."

"Since September. Since he came back from the West."

"And all this time, all these months you kept a secret like this from us? From your parents?"

"A secret like what?" said my father, from the door.

I eased my way to a kitchen chair and sat lightly.

"Like what?" said my father again. My mother motioned toward me, an open hand.

"Tell him," she said. But I couldn't. She stared at me a moment and then spoke herself. "It's Steven," she said. "Les thinks . . . She has reason to think he's not coming. That he's avoiding us because . . ." Dad's blue eyes fastened on me.

"Because he dropped out of school," I said in a small voice. And in the stillness that followed, my words seemed to hang in midair.

My father pulled up a chair opposite me. His eyes bored right through me. "How long have you known?" he said softly.

"Since September." I swallowed hard. "Steve told me when he visited the house. And I know I should have come to you, but I thought . . . I still thought he might change his mind. That maybe I could persuade him. Because he's so smart, really. I couldn't stand seeing him mess up. I even went to visit him once. But I couldn't do anything. Couldn't get him to change his mind. And so I didn't know what to do, whether to tell you or keep quiet."

"You didn't know?" said my father. "You didn't know your responsibilities? To tell your parents when your brother's in serious trouble?"

"He's not in trouble, he's all right. I mean—I saw him and he seemed . . ." Then I thought of his apartment. The mess. The parties. I shut my mouth and sank back in my chair.

"You have a strange sense of values, Leslie. Very strange." My mother shook her head.

"What is he doing, then?" said my father, more to himself than to me. "What's he doing all day there, if he's not going to school? Three whole months have gone by."

"I don't know."

"Three months, and I've been shelling out his money like clockwork. How could he—how dare he abuse me this way?"

There was a long pause. "He wasn't thinking of you," I said softly. "He was trying to figure himself out. To decide . . ."

"Oh, don't give me that crap, I've heard all that before." Dad restlessly passed his hand over the back of his neck. "All this 'finding yourself' garbage, all this discovering your identity. What chance did I have, for luxuries like that? At his age, I was out earning a living. And Steven, with all his advantages, all his opportunities . . ." He lowered his head. "What can you do when a boy wants to throw his life away?"

My mother glanced at me over my father's head. See what you've started? See what you've done? And in a low voice my father went on, the words almost musical, a tune sung to himself.

"His whole life," he murmured. "A whole life he's throwing away. His grades, his sports—the violin that he couldn't bother to practice. One by one we let things go. Every time we start, full of enthusiasm, full of hope, and then—one, two, it's over. It gets a little difficult, boom, it's done. Even the girls, a different one every week. What do I have to hope for from this boy? What?"

"Victor, please." My mother came up timidly behind him and rested her hands on his shoulders. "Don't get worked up, all right? It's not that important, not the end of the world."

"Not important?" He swiveled around to look at her. "Not important that he played me for a fool? That he lied to me, concealed from me? That he abused my trust is not important?"

"Daddy, he was just afraid, he was just—"

"No. No. He thought he was smart, he thought he'd outfox me. Very clever. Like it's for my sake he should get an education. He should make something out of his life." My father shook his head. "He treats me with contempt. Oh, he's happy enough to take my money, take the advantages I've given him. But God forbid I should expect anything in return, any standards. Is it a favor to me he should stay in school? And don't either of you defend him." He rubbed his forehead. "What did I always say," he muttered. "That I didn't want my kids to grow up to work in a hardware store. Hah. With Steven, this would already be an accomplishment."

My mother was crying. Daddy pushed back his chair and walked purposefully out of the kitchen.

"Where are you going?" My mother followed him. "You shouldn't go out in such a state."

"I'm fine, don't worry about me."

"But what are you going to do?"

"Nothing. I'm going out for a walk."

"But dinner will be ready soon."

"You eat it. I need some air."

"We'll wait for you," my mother called from the stoop. "Don't stay out too long." He didn't look back.

Softly she closed the door and turned to me.

"I'm sorry," I whispered. "I'm sorry. Believe me. I never meant this to happen."

"Sooner or later we'd have found out anyway."

"I know but . . . the holiday. All your preparations. If I'd told you before . . ."

"Never mind, Leslie. No one's blaming you." We went together to the living room and sat. Waited there in silence, the rest of the afternoon.

CHAPTER · 12

I T WAS WELL INTO EVENING when my father returned.
At four, my mother took the turkey from the oven and
left it on the stove top to rest. It was shriveled and dry
now. The sweet-potato casserole was brittle around the
edges. We had gone from expectation to letdown with
no stop in between.

My mother got up when he entered, and tried to help
him with his coat. "I can manage," he snapped. He came
into the living room and made a beeline for the liquor
cupboard.

"Rose?" he offered, bottle outstretched.

"No, thanks."

He poured himself a glass of Scotch and put it away
with one swallow. I stared in disbelief. Usually, a single
drink would last him an hour. "So what have you two

done all afternoon?" He stared at us over the rim of his empty glass.

"Nothing. Wait," my mother said.

"For who?"

"You. Who else?"

"Why didn't you start without me?"

"It's a holiday. The family should be together. The best we can." She got up slowly and headed for the kitchen. "I'll get the food," she said. "Victor, you want to carve?"

"Whatever." But he got up and followed behind her. I watched from the dining-room door as my mother set the turkey on the kitchen counter for my father to carve. He pierced the skin with the tip of his knife.

"Beautiful," he said. "Rose, you outdid yourself." He began to sharpen the knife with long, slow strokes against the steel. "Les"—he nodded toward his glass—"get me another drink, would you? Another Scotch."

"But you just had—"

"Do what I say."

My mother turned her back. She began to carry in serving plates—stuffing and gravy and cranberry mold—and set them carefully in the center of the table. Everything was beautiful: the embroidered cloth and festive gold-edged china. But the three place settings looked terribly forlorn. A few minutes later, when my father was done slicing, he carried in the platter of turkey himself and placed it off to one side. Then he reached for the wine. He twisted the corkscrew and it gave way with a muted pop.

"Where are the glasses, Rose? What, only three?"

"What do you mean, three—"

"You don't want to leave one for the prophet Elijah? In case the miracle happens and he shows up?" He filled my glass, but I didn't touch it. "I know you, Rose," he said. "You still expect him, don't you? Steven. You wouldn't give up hope unless he was dead."

"God forbid. Don't even say such a thing."

"Oh, pardon me. You think God's listening? I forget sometimes how much you love your darling boy. Here, allow me," he said, forking a slice of turkey onto my plate. "Such a wonderful meal your mother made. A fatted calf."

"Is it a crime to love your son?" my mother asked.

"Not in all cases." He slapped some turkey on her plate, too, and then sat heavily in his seat. We passed the serving dishes silently. "It's a question of fairness," he said at last. "Balance. Of getting something back."

"Like what?"

"Like . . ." He paused, mulled it over. "I don't mean something back, like money. I mean, like justifying the time spent. The effort. I mean, getting something back in joy."

She hesitated before she spoke, and then her voice was tentative. "Steven gives joy to me," she said. "If he were here, he'd give me joy."

"Oh, to you. What do you know? He eats your chocolate cookies, that gives you joy." He took a long swallow of his wine but didn't touch his food. "The problem with you, Rose," he said, "is you don't discriminate. As far as you're concerned, between Les and Steven there's nothing to choose."

"I love them both," she said.

"Ah, the devoted mother."

"Victor. You make it sound like I'm taking away from her. That if I love Steve, I . . . I don't know. Like there's just so much to go around."

"Well, that's the truth, isn't it? There is only so much. Only twenty-four hours in the day."

My mother's face darkened. "Don't twist things, Victor," she said in a low voice. "I love Leslie as much as you do."

"Love, love. The magic word. But what does it mean, hmm? What are the results? Take a good look at him, Rose. Look at your son and what do you see—a boy who's helpless, who can't do a damn thing or make his way in the world. And now with Les you want more of the same. Always fussing around, treating her like glass. You can't stand the thought of her going out on her own. But I won't allow it, do you hear? I won't let you keep her in a box." He tossed down the rest of his wine. My mother sat very still.

"The music," he went on in a low voice, "Les's music— it never really mattered to you. You think it's a hobby. Busywork. Like, I don't know. Basket weaving. You grudge the time she spends practicing."

She shook her head. "No," said my mother at last. "I only want her to have more to her life. More than just working. She's a young girl—she needs friends, school-work, nice clothes . . ."

"Oh, right, clothes. You and your trips to the mall. Dressing her like a doll." My father snorted. "I'm not talking games here. I'm talking respect. Respect. And I'm the only one that gives that. I'm the only one that listened the first time she picked up the violin. The only one who paid attention, who didn't give up on her, all those months when she was laying on the couch. From the first time I heard her, I knew: this is exceptional. *This* is a gift." He shook his head. "All Leslie does, her hard work, her sacrifice—to you it counts for nothing. And Steve, a boy who sits in his apartment all day, he's your darling. The light of your life."

For a moment she sat rigid in her chair. Then she pushed herself back. "I'll see about tea," she said, and went to the kitchen. My father bent his head over his plate. He flicked the food about with his fork, like a bird searching for bugs under a pile of leaves.

"Why did you do that?" I asked. "Why did you hurt her so? She didn't do anything wrong."

"You came in at the last act," said my father. "There was already a whole play you missed."

The table was spread with the ruins of dinner. I looked at my untouched plate, at the congealed sweet potatoes and the pool of melted Jell-o. And it struck me, suddenly, how that whole conversation had taken place as if I were not there to hear. As if I had no feeling or intelligence. An idiot, or a child.

I got up from the table and headed for the kitchen door.

"Where are you going?" my father asked.

"I don't know. To Mom. Downstairs. My room."

"So you're like her, then? Afraid to hear the truth?"

I pushed on by, into the kitchen. My mother stood at the sink. The water was on hard, cascading over her hands.

"Mom," I said. Her head was lowered, turned away. "Mom . . ."

"I'm all right, Les," she said. "I'll be all right in a minute."

"Can I . . . Is there anything . . ."

"I said I'm all right. It's nothing. Your father's upset. It will pass." I took a step closer to her, ready to put my hand on her shoulder, but thought better of it.

"I'm going to my room," I said. "I want to rest."

In my den it was dark, the early-evening dark of autumn. The drapes and bedspread and woodwork, everything seemed heavy and solid. Immovable. But at least it was quiet and I was alone. I sank wearily on the bed. So it had happened, finally, the blowup I had dreaded so long. All the ugliness out in the open. And nothing was strange, nothing could have been more predictable. Hadn't I heard it a thousand times? That Steve was no good, a bum. That he refused to buckle down, was lazy, squandered his advantages. It was so familiar I could have recited it myself. So why then did it hurt so much? Why had it struck me with such force? I thought back on the other scenes I'd witnessed over the years—my father pacing, his long stride swallowing the room. His white hair raked to stand on end. Steve pink-cheeked, stammering. But as I pictured it in my mind, I realized, suddenly, why this time was different. Steve was gone. He was not here to stumble and blush and melt in a puddle of uncertainty. But the song—my father's song—had played on.

All these years, my father had said the punishments were for Steve's own good. And trusting, I believed him. What a fool! Steve's good was never the issue. All that mattered was Victor—his ambitions, his goals. His disappointment. It made no difference that Steve was gone, because my father never saw him when he was here. He saw only what Steve was not—what he lacked, what he could never be. But the gentle, funny, easy boy I knew— my father never looked at him.

How it must have been for Steve, living in this house! Struggling to be—what? Who could tell, when no one had let him be himself? Even I had not loved him as he was—so smug and superior I'd been. I thought of Jeff in his room. The rows of science-fiction paperbacks and the dozens of Matchbox cars on their open shelves. Would he have played with those toys in this house? Would they have been permitted? And what about me? Wasn't it, after all, just my good luck that what came easy to me was the thing my father loved? That his dreams were also my own?

That night, I lay awake for a long time, thinking. The room was pitch-dark, the curtains drawn tight. And I had shut and locked the door to the upstairs. The only glow came from the luminous panel of the clock on my dresser, and all night I watched the numbers change, my eyes dry and wide open. At four o'clock I gave up trying to sleep. I sat on the edge of the bed and dressed and went to the outside door that opens on the garden. It was chilly but not biting cold, dark but not as dark as my room. There was a hazy, cloud-veiled moon overhead that I could see through the bare branches of the trees. The trees draw themselves inward, I thought. They drop their soft leaves when winter comes. As they must.

My brother was gone. Gone in his own way, by the back door—sneaking off without a word. As always, afraid. I missed him already, my Steve, so playful and funny. Missed him, but could not wish him back. Because I did not trust my father. And if you cannot trust your father and mother to love you and accept you and protect you, then you are an orphan, although your parents are upstairs asleep in their bed.

CHAPTER · 13

I STAYED OUT IN THE COLD until the sky lightened, just past six o'clock. Then, feeling hungry, I went inside. I got some cereal from the kitchen and brought it to my room and ate it dry, right out of the box, until it was all gone. And with my stomach taut with food, sleep overcame me all at once, as if a narcotic had taken effect.

I slept until nine. There was a knock on the door then, a shy knock: my mother's.

"Leslie, sweetheart," she sang out. "Are you awake?"

I sat up. My mouth had a sour leftover taste; I ran my tongue over my dry rough teeth. My clothes were crumpled with sleep.

"What is it?"

"I'm sorry to disturb you. Your friend's here. Jeffrey," she added.

I tried to collect myself. "I'm coming," I called. I ran my fingers through my hair and smoothed my clothing. I had to think hard for a moment to be certain what day it was. Jeff was at his grandmother's, wasn't he? But no, that was yesterday.

I hastily brushed my teeth and went up the two steps to the kitchen, carefully shutting my door behind me. Jeff was at the table, drinking orange juice.

"What are you doing here?" I asked stupidly.

"Nothing. I just came to see you. We got back last night and I . . . Les, are you okay? You look funny."

My mother stood up from the table. "I was just on my way upstairs," she said with obvious tact. "You children go ahead and talk, help yourselves if you want something. I was just going to make the bed." She backed out.

"Gosh, she's really trying," said Jeff. "She'll be like my mother soon."

I sat down heavily across from him. I poured myself a glass of juice and drank it. My mouth was very dry.

"I didn't sleep," I said. "I was awake all night."

"How come?"

For a moment, I thought of explaining. "Yesterday, we . . ." I shook my head. The familiarity of the house was smothering me, like a cloth over my face.

"Leslie, what is it?"

"I can't." I stood. "Not here. Jeffrey, let's get out. I don't care where, but I can't stay." I was already halfway to the door and Jeff had to scurry to catch up.

We got in the car and drove. I didn't tell Jeff where to go, I couldn't think that clearly. I leaned my elbow on the door and hid my face there. Slowly I realized that Jeff was taking us to the shore, to the beach where Steve and I had always gone, as if he had some eerie clair-voyance.

"Jeffrey, why did you pick this place? How did you know?"

"Know what?"

"Never mind. Nothing."

We drove through the tacky, weather-beaten village and parked near the beach. The huge lot, overflowing in summer, was empty now. The sky was low, the wind from the ocean steady and sharp with salt. I climbed up the ramp to the boardwalk and looked out at the sand, littered with broken shells and blackened clumps of seaweed. Far off was a woman walking a dog, but otherwise the beach was deserted; no one was near. The wind buffeted us, and I held the railing for support.

"Steve was right," I said softly. My words were almost swallowed in the breeze. "Everything he said was right, and I was wrong."

Jeff came closer, leaning in to hear. "You never told me what he said. Steve. What was he right about?" I didn't answer. "What happened yesterday?" asked Jeff. "Did he tell your parents?"

"He didn't tell. He never came. Jeff, he never showed, he never even called."

He paused a moment to take it in. "So, what happened, then?"

"What happened? I told them. I had to, I couldn't let it go on. My mother, she'd made this huge feast and . . . God, Jeff. If you had seen her face. How it dropped."

"It must have been rough."

"Yes. Although—strange as it sounds—I think Steve wanted me to tell. Deep down, I think he knew he'd never have the nerve. He wanted me to help him."

"But you feel guilty, anyway? Is that the idea? For being the one . . ."

"No." I shook my head. "No guilt. Or at least not for that."

I started down the boardwalk toward the arcades. All the honky-tonk was closed up tight for winter. The taffy stands and video-game parlors. The restaurants with their odors of french fries and greasy clams. I found a bench that faced the sea and sat, carefully, steadying myself with my hands. Jeff eased in gingerly beside me. He took my hand, and I took it back.

"I came to this beach with Steve," I said. "Many times. Just this fall, when he told me his news. But before that, with the family, when we were children. Until he was fourteen, fifteen. And he'd help me swim. I'd unstrap my legs and he would carry me. He'd hold me in his arms and take me out in the water, where it was shallow and warm, and I would just float. Close my eyes. So light. The sun on my face." I broke off. For a moment I could not master my voice.

Then I said, "I couldn't bear to tell you, what Steve said that day. I thought, if I never said it, never repeated it—I didn't want it to be true. Jeff, do you remember, in your room? When you tried—you wanted to kiss me? And I wouldn't do it. I said no without even thinking."

"It was my fault. It was stupid of me. You were upset and worried—of course you weren't in the mood."

"No." I shook my head. "It wasn't the timing. It was the idea of someone touching me. Steve"—I held up my hand to stop him interrupting—"Steve said I was a saint. That I had no human urges. That I didn't know what pleasure was. Whether it was candy or . . . it sounds so crude, doesn't it?" I blushed. "Of course, when Steve said it, I didn't believe him. He just wanted to make himself out as wicked, the opposite of me. So he could say it was out of his control, that there was no way he could be good. Could win my father's love. And naturally I argued with him; I didn't want to think that. But now— now I'm not sure anymore. Because the way my father talked yesterday—talked about both of us—I began to see what Steve meant. That it *is* easy for me and hard for him. To do the right thing. Somehow, I got a taste of what he must feel, and I knew it must be true that Steve can't change. Because he wouldn't suffer like that if he could help it."

The waves made a steady roar in the distance, but my eyes were down and I couldn't see that far away. I felt Jeff lean close beside me and brush his hand to my cheek. Brush back the hair, as the wind did. And I saw also his cramped legs, his feet dangling, pointed toe-to-toe.

"Is that what you think?" he asked. "That Steve is right? That somehow you're different from everyone else on earth, you don't have the same feelings as the rest of us? Or maybe you think that's what being good is? Being all locked up inside and afraid to come out?"

I shook my head. Tears had filled my eyes and my throat was too knotted to talk.

"Oh, Leslie," he whispered. "You're so smart, and you're so dumb. You believe some half-baked theory of your brother's, but you don't trust your own feelings. You're scared, Les. That's all that's wrong with you: you're scared. Well, so what? Who isn't? How do you think I feel, sitting here next to you?"

I moved a fraction of an inch and his arms came around me. He kissed me, half-on, half-off the lips, and then we stood and he pulled me closer, although his legs made an awkward angle, so his body could not quite meet my own. The ocean breeze whipped at us; I felt unsteady and near to losing my balance.

"Let's go out of the wind," he whispered. "Down on the sand."

We picked our way down a short flight of wooden steps. There, in the lee of the jetty, in a sheltered place between the boardwalk and the rocks, we lay together. Jeff covered us with his coat, to shield us from the damp. Now I could feel his body, his thin fragile bones, and against my hip that part of him, hard and straight, a thick rope. He kissed me, long kisses that made it hard to swallow or even breathe, but that might have been fright, or exhilaration. His breath stirred against my neck, warm, but his hands were cold. They left a trail of goose bumps on my skin. And then he slid his hand beneath my blouse and I stiffened, and he whispered, "Let me." And I remembered sitting at the ocean's edge as a child, and feeling the sand tugged from beneath me, sucked away by the waves. Let it go, I thought. Can't hold it. Let it go. And on my face the sea air was damp, salty, restless.

"What time is it?" I said at last.

Jeff rustled, gently maneuvered me aside to check his watch. "One."

"Oh, my God. I have to leave."

He nodded and rose clumsily, then helped me to my feet. Without much success, he tried to repair his dishevelment—pulling out his shirttails and smoothing his jacket on top.

"How do I look?" I asked.

"Beautiful."

"No, I mean . . ."

He shook his head. "You're fine."

We climbed back up the stairs and returned as we came, down the boardwalk. A few joggers were out now, and they smiled as they passed us.

"How did you know?" I asked. "You knew me better than I did."

"Do you remember the time in your father's store? When I came in, and you had that box of paper dolls."

"Oh God, that. I felt so foolish."

"But I liked you foolish. I liked seeing you play."

He helped me into the car and we left for home. I didn't think much, as we drove—not in the usual sense. I thought with my gut, the pit of my stomach. The dry catch in my throat. An enveloping amazement that what had happened had happened. The length of his body against mine. How hard he was, under his clothes. I never knew it would be so obvious. Between my legs was a melting slipperiness. I leaned back in my seat. About one thing Steve had been wrong. I was not a freak, or a saint. And sweeter even than the physical pleasure was the relief of being at last free of the weight of all that virtue.

CHAPTER · 14

FOR THE REMAINDER OF THE WEEKEND, I wandered in a daze. Bobbie called, we made polite chitchat, but I wasn't ready yet to share what I felt. I wanted to hoard it for myself. Later Jeff phoned—but what could I say to him? What would be enough but not too much? I was filled with delicious betrayals; I felt at any moment I might give myself away. That my body could give me pleasure astonished me. Thinking back on it, all I could remember was pain. Doctors and nurses prodding, ill-fitting prostheses, straps that gave friction burns, and skin that was tender, or else too thick to feel. Even the idea that one could create pleasure for oneself had always been abstract to me. God knows I'd never done such a thing, never discussed it even with my best friend.

Now I wondered where I had been all these years. It was as if I'd dropped down the rabbit hole into Wonderland.

The following Monday, Bobbie met me at the bus stop. She looked sleepy and unwilling to go back.

"How was your weekend?" I asked.

"Fattening." She squinted at me. "How was yours?"

I shook my head. I'd have to explain it some other time. When she had an hour or two to spare.

At the other end of the ride, Jeff was waiting. I spotted him as I stepped off the bus: gangly, redheaded, sporting a grin. He waved to me from the broad school stairs, and my stomach flip-flopped. I took a deep steadying breath, then smiled and waved back. I excused myself from Bobbie.

"Hi, Les," he said, shuffling. He took a step toward me, as if to kiss or hug, then transformed the gesture. "Allow me," he said with a slight flourish, and took my violin. "How was your weekend?"

"I think you know, Jeffrey."

"I meant the rest of it."

"Was there a rest of it?"

He swung the violin case lightly as he walked. "Thought I'd catch you early," he said. "See if you wanted my company today. In the practice room at lunch."

"Yes, I would." Then I paused. "On second thought— maybe we could eat in the lunchroom today. You could meet my friends." I blushed as I said it. He was so goofy-looking, with that long red hair. That swishy walk. What would they think of him? I was already starting to regret the idea.

"Hey, that sounds great. Just imagine, I get to sit at an entire table full of attractive girls."

And so at lunch we descended on Bobbie and her crew. My friend was surprised but welcoming. She squeezed me in beside her, across from Celeste and her buddies. Jeff sat next to me; Eric was on Bobbie's other side. There were introductions all around. And then, to my embarrassment, Jeff launched into one of his routines. Oh no, I thought. Not this again. But of course they hadn't heard it before.

"Hmm, what have we here?" he said, as he unwrapped his lunch. "Rye bread, a bad sign." He peeled open the sandwich and sniffed. "Les, you think I should trust salami?" Bobbie gave him an amused and skeptical glance.

"Is something wrong?" she asked.

"What? Oh no. Just my mother's cooking. She's very involved with her career and all, and so she sometimes neglects these little domestic . . ." He took another peek beneath the bread. "I never know what to expect with her. She has one of those fridges—you know the kind? Full of mysterious packages covered in green mold. I'm always afraid something will leap out at me. But I'll have to chance it." He took a bite. "Hmm, not bad. It's fairly safe, really, if you use common sense. You know, things like: never eat anything with mayonnaise, and go with peanut butter toward the end of the week."

Everyone laughed. I gave Bobbie a nervous look and she squeezed close to me. "He's cute," she whispered.

"Thank you," I whispered back. Then, to the table, I said, "I thought she looked so sweet, Jeff. Your mother. Now I find out she's trying to murder you."

"Not murder, just manslaughter. Unintentional."

By that time, I'd unwrapped my sandwich. I took a hefty bite.

"Leslie's mother," said Bobbie, "is just the opposite. House Beautiful. You could eat off the floor."

"Oh, but she's got her own problems," I said. "She recycles. You know? She makes a roast, and then makes hash out of the leftovers, and then makes shepherd pie out of the hash. Toward the end, you get this sort of permanent *déjà vu*."

It was like a miracle. As if we'd been a gang our whole lives. When we finished eating, Jeff and I went to dump our trash.

"You like them?" I said.

"They're very nice." And as I smiled and flushed with pleasure, Jeff leaned over and murmured in my ear. "Leslie. Has it occurred to you—since we seem to be an item now—that we might go on a date?"

"What do you mean?"

"A date. You know? What boys and girls do? Go out some evening and see a movie. Play miniature golf."

"Miniature *golf*? You're kidding." But he wasn't kidding, not about the invitation. I hesitated. "You know, Jeff, I never told you, but—I've never gone on a date before. Never, not once."

"So what? You've been doing lots of new things recently."

And so it was decided. Friday, the movies. I checked it with my mom and got her blessing. She was enthusiastic, actually. I, on the other hand, was a wreck of anticipation. That evening, before he arrived, was a nightmare. Dinner was absolutely silent—forty-five minutes, from grapefruit to goulash to tea and cake, and no one said a word. Afterwards, I went to my room to dress—another fiasco. I must have spent an hour choosing an outfit, trying things on and tossing them aside, until my place looked like a fitting room at Bloomingdale's. I knew it was ridiculous, he saw me every day in my regular school clothes, but I couldn't stop myself. Finally I settled on a pair of loose gray pants and a sweater, with one of my mother's silk scarves to tone things up.

And at 7:30 the doorbell rang.

Jeff, to his credit, was a model of good behavior. First he told me how lovely I looked. Then he gave a bow to my mother and dad. Mom bubbled all over him, she was more excited than I was. But my father barely raised his eyes from the *Times*. After these preliminaries, Jeff took me by the elbow and escorted me very gallantly to the car. He acted as if the little Gumdrop was Cinderella's coach. Once inside, we put the radio on to some funky rock and roll and Jeff started keeping time with the beat. Flapping his wings, actually, since his feet were occupied. The station went in for oldies, most of which I'd never heard before. But of course I wasn't much up on rock and roll. It wasn't turned up excessively loud, and I began to see how people might like the stuff, the looseness of it. Even if it did lack the intellectual subtlety of the Bach Chaconne.

We sped away to the theater, and the whole thing, every minute of it, was fun—even standing outside in the cold for fifteen minutes, waiting for the doors to open. It was one of those big multi-movie palaces, all red carpets and mirrors. I glanced around once or twice to see if anyone noticed us, how different we looked, but it was so crowded, no one saw. The air in the lobby was dense, the smell of buttered popcorn overpowering. We walked past the movie posters and concession stand with its boxes of nonpareils and jujubes.

"You know," I said, "I think the last movie I saw was *The Lady and the Tramp.* Can you imagine how long it's been?"

"Not hardly. What have you been doing for fun all this time?"

"Nothing." I said, and laughed.

The movie itself I don't remember well. I was too aware of the experience, the newness of it, to pay attention to the story. I sat goggle-eyed, like a kid watching cartoons. Staring at Tom Cruise. God, he was handsome. Sexy. Jeff laced his fingers in mine and our hands rested together gently. I glanced at him from the corner of my eye. Thought about our drive home. What we would do then. How it would feel.

When the movie ended, we went out the side entrance into the cold night.

"You want to go for a bite to eat, or some dessert? There's a Friendly's across the street."

"No, thanks, I'm not hungry."

"Straight home, then? Or . . ."

Or. He drove me home but parked halfway down the block. It was dark except for the streetlight on the corner, and warm in the car, from the long drive.

"You know how I felt tonight?" I said. "Like a teenager out of a TV sitcom. Gidget goes to the Malt Shop."

"So? Is that so bad? You're entitled, Leslie, you are a teenager. For two more years, anyway. And you've got a lot of catching up to do."

"It took me long enough, didn't it? To realize I wanted to catch up."

"Yes. You're my Sleeping Beauty." He caught my hand and pressed it to his cheek. And I felt it, that slipping away. How wonderful it was. I shook my head.

"Oh, Jeff. When I think of the grief I gave poor Bobbie. All those put-downs. I can't believe I acted like such a snob." And I realized then what that sweet taste was in my mouth, that light feeling in my head. It was normalcy. That intoxicating wine. And, oh, was I drunk.

CHAPTER · 15

A FEW WEEKS LATER, I came back late from a date and found my father waiting up.

It had been a strange time for my father. While I was busy with my own life, which seemed suddenly to be blooming and expanding in all directions, my father had been shrinking into himself. In a sense, you could say he didn't change, that his lifelong pattern simply deepened, like the lines on a person's face as he grows older. He'd always eaten little; now he seemed to live on nothing at all. Always early to work and late home, now he lived at the store. Sometimes two or three days would pass without my seeing him. And when he was around, he was transparent, motionless, silent. Sitting in the armchair, eyes ahead, headphones playing Mahler or Beethoven. Turning the pages of the newspaper, too quickly to be taking in the words. But tonight, as I opened the front door, he looked up from his newspaper and stared at me with his watery blue eyes.

"Daddy," I said, surprised. "I thought you'd be upstairs by now."

"Why, what time is it?" He consulted his watch dreamily. "Twelve-fifteen. Yes, I guess I should be in bed. But I was waiting."

"For me?"

"Of course. Who else?" He sat forward slightly in his seat. "Where were you so late?"

"Out with friends. I told you at dinner, don't you remember?"

"No. What friends?"

"Bobbie and Eric. Jeff." I half swallowed the word, hoping to slip it by.

"Where did you go?"

"Just out. Daddy, unless there's something you want . . . I'm tired. Do you think we could talk in the morning?"

"I won't keep you long." He patted the chair beside his. "Come sit down. You want tea? I have tea, I can make you a cup."

I shook my head. I couldn't figure out what he was after. He was moving in a kind of slow motion and seemed quite willing to sit up with me all night. I sat across from him and watched him raise the cup, sip loudly, lower the cup.

"I've been thinking," he said.

"What about?"

"Oh, many things. Past and future. This house, for instance. When we bought it, Steve was five years old. You were a baby, we had you in a little nursery upstairs.

That tiny room, we use it for storage now. Do you remember?" I shook my head. "Well, I suppose not. Just books and boxes in there now. Your mother's sewing machine. And Steve's room empty, too. Pretty soon the whole house will be empty. Next year, when you're off to school."

I nodded. Settled back in my chair. He just wanted to talk, perhaps. Maybe he'd go on like this to anyone who wandered in.

"You know, it's so hard to predict," he said. "You start with a baby, and you watch it grow. Maybe it talks early, or likes to climb on the table. It's quiet or it's loud—anyway, you get a notion, this is the personality. The child's like this or like that—you follow me?" I nodded. "And so, sometimes you see it going a certain way, telling fibs maybe, or too shy, hanging on the mother's skirt, and you say to yourself, 'Now, I'll step in and fix this. Can't have this.' And you do. You try. But then the child grows up and nothing's like you expected, and you wonder, did I do this, did I handle it wrong? Or maybe it would have happened anyway, maybe it was in the genes."

I yawned. "I'm sorry," I said quickly. "I'm sleepy."

"It's all right, I bore myself." He held up his hand. "Let's talk about something else. You're interesting, let's talk about you."

"What's interesting about me?"

"What do you mean, how can you say such a thing? You're my princess, I care about everything you do. Tell me, how is the concerto coming? The Mendelssohn, right? That's going to be important, the concerto, that counts at the audition."

"It's coming all right." Actually, I wanted to say, it's

all important—the scales, the études, every damn note matters. And I don't want to think about it now.

"I haven't heard you lately," he said. "I miss it."

"You've been getting home late. Also, I practice at school a lot."

"Yes, my fault, I know. But how is it? Is your teacher pleased?"

"As far as I know. Well, she wants me to perform more, we always argue about that, but—"

"That's good, that's good. Because I know Miss Rosenzweig's a perfectionist. If she didn't like your work, she'd let you know." His voice trailed off. "Where did you say you went tonight?"

"I didn't say. It wasn't anyplace special, just out with Jeff."

"Jeff. Jeff. Do I know him?"

"Daddy! Of course you know him, he came to the house. Don't you remember? You met him at the store, that day? The one with the red hair . . ."

"Oh, yes. With the legs."

"That's right." I felt a tingle in my cheeks. "Do you have to put it that way, 'with the legs'? Everyone has legs—except me, of course. And if you mean the one with the crooked legs, the limp, you don't have to say that, either."

"What?" He looked up, bewildered. "Did I say something wrong?"

"Oh, never mind." I shook my head. "Daddy, I've got to go to bed, I'm exhausted."

"What? Oh yes." He jumped, looked at his watch. "Of course, sweetheart, I'm keeping you up. You get some rest. Tomorrow is a new day."

I was grateful to go to my room. What a strange little

interview. What was he after, what did he want? He'd never talked this way to me before. It was not how a parent talks to a child; it was open, somehow, unguarded. His air of authority misplaced. Besides, he'd mentioned Steve for the first time since Thanksgiving. Was it perhaps a sign of softening? Was he getting ready to make peace? And if so, what would Steve think of it? I'd wondered about him off and on, these past weeks. How he was getting along. According to my mother, Daddy never went to see him after the big scene. He'd written a note to say his support was cut—a note, of all things. It seemed the farthest limit of insult.

In the bathroom, I readied myself for bed. Washed and changed to my nightgown. As I slipped it on, I ran my hands over my breasts. I liked it when Jeff touched me there. Weeks later, the pleasure was still a surprise. Then, at my bedside, I unstrapped my legs and slipped between the sheets. All this talk tonight with my father about music—what a lot of lies. I hadn't worked during lunch in weeks. Even my evening sessions had grown shorter. It was no accident, his not hearing me. But what I'd said about Elli was true enough. She hadn't mentioned anything, hadn't seemed displeased. I was sure she could hear the difference, the lack of precision and crispness in my playing: I could. Not that I sounded bad, yet. Just not as good as I could be.

I rolled over toward the wall. What was happening to me? Was it just the distraction, the lovely world I'd discovered, luring me from my work? Old hat, somehow, to be so adolescent. For so long, music had defined my life. Was it possible that, after all this time, my interest was fading? And if I stopped caring for music, what then? What else would I do?

The next Wednesday, a cold mid-December afternoon, I went as usual for my lesson. My mother dropped me on the doorstep of Elli's old brownstone, and I rang the bell.

"So." My teacher greeted me with a dry kiss on both cheeks. "It's my budding virtuosa. I'm pleased to see that so far you still remember the way to the front door. Come in." She ushered me into the living room and sat me on the threadbare Louis XIV couch. Then she disappeared into the kitchen.

"I was just making tea," she called. "I thought you might like a cup." I heard the clink of china.

"I'm not thirsty, Elli." But she didn't listen. In a moment she came back with the tea tray. "This neighborhood is getting so fancy," she said. "Look at these cookies I bought down the street. Seven dollars a pound, do you believe it? Here, have one."

"You'll ruin my appetite, I have dinner in a couple of hours . . ."

"Oh, go on," she said. "You're young, you'll manage. Don't make me eat them all." She set the tray down on the table in front of me and I took one and bit in. They were wonderful cookies, buttery. Big chunks of chocolate.

"Do you remember when I used to give you chocolates?" she asked. "When you first started here? That bonbon dish?"

"How could I forget it?"

"You drove me crazy, fumbling around with them. Couldn't make up your mind."

"No, it wasn't that. I was scared of you."

She turned to me with her clear, level glance. "Scared of me? Not anymore, I hope?"

"Of course not."

"Well. That's good." She nodded. "Because then, you see, I can ask you straight, without a lot of beating around the bush. What it is you think you're doing, these past weeks. What kind of game you're playing with your music."

So. At last. I didn't get as far as an answer. All I did was open my mouth.

"Oh, come on, Leslie, come, come. Don't get embarrassed. I'm an old lady, I've been around the block. I can hear what's happening. Unless you think maybe I'm going deaf?"

I felt a flush rise in my cheeks. My hands got sweaty and the remnant chocolate-chip cookie started to melt. "Is it that bad?" I asked in a low voice. "I know I've been slacking a little, but . . ."

"Bad? No, not bad. You're a good musician, you can fake. But I'm good too, I know fake from real. You're only playing at playing. Your mind is elsewhere. You're not paying attention to what you do."

I sighed. There really was no sense in trying to conceal it. "I have a boyfriend," I said at last.

"So?" She leaned back in her seat. "Mazel tov. What's his name?"

"Jeff Penner."

"A nice name. A nice boy?" I nodded, mutely. "So what's the problem?"

I didn't answer. Elli lit a cigarette and the smoke plumed above her like a cloud. "Love," she said. "It's wonderful, no? I'm jealous. But I thought you did this before now."

"No. It's the first time."

"Ah. I begin to see. It's the old story, then. A girl starts dating, running around . . . Next thing, the music is out the window. Every teacher knows this scenario."

"I'm sorry I'm not more original."

"What? Oh, don't be. This is part of life. Something you ought to do." She ground out her cigarette. "Of course," she went on, "for you, with your talent, I'd hate for this to become a permanent situation. It doesn't have to be, you know. Music and life can coexist."

"What?"

"What I mean is, Leslie, you don't have to be a nun. I don't consider this a reasonable request. But"—she looked at me meaningfully—"you do need to work harder. To make room for both. It takes an extra effort, now."

I sighed. I put down the last morsel of cookie and wiped my fingers on a napkin.

"Here." She moistened a hankie in tea and passed it to me. "You missed some spots." While I dabbed, she regarded me thoughtfully. "I've been wondering what your father thinks about all this," she said at last. "Your love life. He approves?"

"I couldn't say. To tell the truth, he's been sort of weird, lately. Wrapped up in himself. He doesn't seem to notice anything that's going on."

"Why is that? Is there some problem?"

"It's my brother. You remember him, right? But this time he took it a little far, I mean, he got Daddy very upset."

"What did he do? Is he in jail?"

"Oh no, nothing like that. He dropped out of college."

"Ah, I see. Your father would take this very much to heart. He cares a great deal about his children. About their accomplishments."

"You can say that again."

"Yes. And about you especially he cares. I know because Sunday he called me. He had the desire to talk."

"What about?"

"Your music, of course. How you're coming along."

"And what did you say to him?"

"I told him you were doing fine." She didn't miss a beat as she said it.

"Thank you," I whispered.

She shrugged. "I don't expect my reassurance to satisfy him for long. He's a smart man, your father. Not so much formal training, but a good ear. Don't forget how he noticed your talent in the cradle. And you know what Paderewski said, don't you? 'If I miss practicing for one day, I notice it; if I miss two days, the critics notice it; three days and the audience notices it.' Where your playing is concerned, your father is at least as sharp as the critic from the *Times*."

For a moment, I had to cover my face. Never, never had Elli needed to speak like this to me. As if I were a stumbling schoolchild who had to be coaxed or wheedled to play. I had never needed urging.

Elli saw the gesture. She reached across and gave me a feathery pat on the arm. "Leslie, forget it, it's nothing. This happens to everyone, sooner or later. The violin—there's a lot of sacrifice involved. And not all of it is made so easily."

I got up and went to the window and looked out at the familiar street. The gray weathered cement of the sidewalk, the brownstones beyond. Soon my mother would circle around the block and wait for me. Ready to drive me back home. To shuttle me, safe in the car, down Broadway. Past the shops and bustle and lights.

"Elli," I murmured. "Do you realize—can you believe—I've never walked down Broadway? How many years have I been coming here? But every week I go back and forth in the car. Like in a bubble. Watching through the glass."

"It's not so wonderful. A lot of noise and dirt."

"You take it for granted. You don't appreciate how wonderful it is. To be able to walk out there, go wherever you want. Turn down this street or that one. Decide for yourself."

There was a long pause. "So?" she said softly. "You feel boxed in? You want to go free? If you think the music is tying you down, then forget it, give it up. You have my permission: go. Fly like a bird."

"No, Elli, it's not the music. It's . . ." I took a long moment, searching my thoughts. "I wish my father hadn't called you."

"He was just concerned."

But I knew better. It was more than mere concern. And suddenly I thought of Steve at the violin. How his face always flushed and his lip grew sweaty with effort and shame. All the hard work of failure. And in the background always—my father. Listening. Wherever he was in the house, whatever else he did, he was always alert to pounce on any fault or weakness, any quavering in attack or pitch. Or devotion.

"Did he say anything else?" I asked. "Did you talk a long time?"

"Oh, he had some questions. He asked about your repertoire, the audition requirements."

"What did you tell him about those things? All the technical stuff?"

"I put him off. It's not his business, really. He wants

to express concern, interest, that's fine. But the details, technical matters—that's my affair, not his."

But then I remembered my father's grilling of my brother this past fall. That long, humiliating discussion of Steve's imaginary major. I doubted my father would agree that the details were not his affair.

Elli finished the last of her tea. "Leslie, it's late. We're talking all afternoon here. Don't you want to play a little?"

But I stood motionless by the window. I saw now that my father had been sleeping these past weeks. Lost in himself. Whatever he felt about Steve—some sense of loss, or disappointment—had blinded him for a short while to his surroundings. So he hadn't noticed my goings-on, my dates and talks on the telephone. My friendship with Jeff. Now the old lion was waking and starting to prowl. He was hungry—and it was to me he'd come—for the joy that nourished his soul. He would come to his angel and ask her to play. But I was through with pleasing. Done with being good and earning favor. If Steve could not have it, why should I? I would not play for him. If he wanted to hear the violin, he could do as others do; he could put down his money and go hear Perlman at Carnegie Hall.

CHAPTER · 16

THAT NIGHT AT DINNER, my father's eyes were bright. And though as always he ate and spoke little, there was purpose in his movements. He was finished mourning.

My mother passed the serving plates, baked chicken and lima beans. "So, Leslie," she asked, "how was your lesson today?"

I looked up. Strange, the question coming from her. I wondered if the two of them had worked it out in advance. But her face was smooth and innocent.

"Fair," I answered.

I lowered my head and picked at my food. Elli's sweets had spoiled my appetite. Or something had. I glanced at the clock on the kitchen wall, wishing it was not too early to be excused.

"What did you work on?" my father asked.

"We . . ." I stopped. We hadn't worked at all. We had talked, and that talk had led nowhere I wanted my father to go. But I couldn't bring myself to lie bald-faced.

"How's the Mendelssohn coming along?" he went on. "That should be your big piece, right? Your concerto. I'd like to hear it one of these days. It's been a long time since I heard you play."

"You've been busy a lot, Victor," said my mother gently. "Les finishes before you get home."

"She never used to finish so early. She used to go till eight, nine o'clock."

There was a long poised silence in the room. In my mind I saw the image of a balance tipping back and forth. Which way would it go? It teetered.

"I can't play for you tonight," I said steadily. "I have plans."

"Homework?" asked my mother.

"Not exactly. I was going to see Jeff."

"On a Wednesday? A school night?"

I had no plans, no arrangements made. I didn't even know if he was free. I prayed he was, though, prayed I wouldn't have to shame myself by backing down.

"We're going out to study," I said. My voice even, but my cheeks hot. "To the library."

"Now you tell me. Why didn't you say so earlier?"

"Aren't you seeing an awful lot of this boy?" asked my father. "All of a sudden?"

I didn't move. I sat still. I drew in breath and it lodged under my ribs and stayed there.

"I like him," I said. "He likes me."

"But, Les," my mother remonstrated. "Tonight . . .

you're tired, you had your lesson. There's school in the morning . . ."

"Excuse me." I pushed back my chair. As near as I could manage, I ran to my room. Shut and locked the door. Then, shaky, I called Jeff's number. And thank God he was there and could come. I went out the back door and waited in the garden for him. My coats were all upstairs, all I had was a sweater. And it was a cold night. I shivered under the stars.

Finally, I heard his car on the street. I hurried out to meet him and yanked open the door.

"Hey, what's with you?" he said. I swung my legs in awkwardly. The little Gumdrop was chilly and running rough, in sudden jerks and coughs. The smell of exhaust seeped in the windows. "More trouble on the home front?" he asked.

"Yes. More of the same. Same old shit."

He blinked in surprise. "You *are* upset." He hesitated. "Well . . . where do you want me to go, then? You have something special in mind?"

"Just . . . I don't know, Jeff. Park somewhere. Maybe we can find some privacy."

We drove a few blocks and parked on a quiet dead-end street. It grew cold inside quickly. Suddenly I wanted him to touch me. I slid closer, clumsy on the rough up-holstered seat, and tried to reach my hands around his neck, to draw him toward me for a kiss. But I missed somehow and knocked his chin. I took a breath. Well, at least I wasn't hampered with a heavy coat. I slipped beneath my sweater and unfastened my bra. Guided his hand.

"Hey, Les. Wait a minute, all right? Just slow down."

"Maybe we could go in back." I looked searchingly at the rear seat. "There's more room, I could sort of stretch out."

"Les. Just stop it, will you? Stop."

He flicked on the dome light.

It was backwards, damn it. Everyone knew. Boys are supposed to want it all the time. Girls go along to please. Yet there he sat, nonchalant, his hand draped over the steering wheel.

"Oh, hell," I said, and began to straighten my clothing. If he didn't even care.

"Leslie," he said gently. "What has gotten into you tonight? Have you lost your mind? Talk to me."

"I don't have anything to say. Anything pleasant."

"Why not? Are you mad at me?"

But no, of course I wasn't mad at him. I was mad at my father, mad at the injustice of the world. I was filled to the back teeth with anger. Not mad at Jeff. It just slopped over onto him.

"I'm sorry," I muttered. "It's not your fault."

"Why don't you tell me about it from the beginning."

But the beginning, where was that? So long ago I could barely remember. My childhood, my seventh year. The moment when, lying helpless on the couch, I picked up my brother's violin and stroked the bow across the strings. Felt the vibration pulse through me. The excitement, the sense of power. The joy. But also what came right after. My father calling, "Rose, come here! Come quick! Look at Les, playing the violin." His joy, as great as my own. His pride and delight.

How could I explain it? That he owned me, and I would

no longer be owned. That the music pleased him, and I wanted not to please. I turned to Jeff, and my eyes were full. Everything shimmered.

I said, "He called my teacher. He called behind my back."

"So?"

"He spied on me. He wanted to check up. Why? Why does he have to interfere?"

"I don't understand, Les. He's concerned, you know that. He's always loved your music."

"No. This isn't love. This is . . ." I shook my head. Elli is mine, I wanted to say. My lessons are my own. But he wants to take it for himself. What will he tell me next— whether to play forte or piano? What tempo to choose?

"Les." Jeff reached for my hand. His fingers were soft, so surpassingly gentle on mine. I pulled away.

"I don't want to play!" I shouted. "Do you understand? I don't want to play anymore."

"You don't mean that."

"Oh, but I do. You don't know how I do. Ever since Thanksgiving—when I saw him the way he really is. Jeff, you know what's been happening with me. I haven't been practicing much lately. I've been skipping lunch sessions, putting in less time at night. I thought it was because of you—I mean, us. But it's not distraction. I didn't realize till now. It's deliberate, Jeff. Some part of me. I'm fed up. Too fed up to play."

He leaned his head on the steering wheel. "I don't believe this, Leslie. I don't believe I'm hearing this."

"Why not? Don't I have reason to be angry?"

"So go ahead, be angry. But not this way. For Pete's sake, Les. Music is your life. I can understand your getting sidetracked—temporarily—but stopping? Quitting? I can't believe you'd consider it."

"Wait and see."

"I don't want to. I don't want to see it ever. And to do it out of spite, Les. It's so . . ." He straightened and pulled his arms in close across his chest. "You'd better think this over. Don't do anything hasty."

"It's already done. My mind's made up. Jeff, it's my decision."

"Fine. Your decision. But leave me out of it, all right? I don't want anything to do with you screwing up your life."

We sat a moment longer in the cold darkness. Then he started the car.

"It's because of Steve," I said at last. "What my father said that night. It made me see. He doesn't love me for myself, Jeffrey. Only for my playing. For the pretty music I make."

But whether he believed or disbelieved, he didn't say. He leaned forward and checked the mirror and pulled out the car. Without another word, he drove me the few blocks back to my house and in silence dropped me off.

I came in through the garden, the back way. I didn't want to see anyone, least of all my father. But the door to the upstairs, which I had locked, was ajar. He had opened it while I was gone. And when he heard me enter he came and stood in the doorway, looming over me.

"Where have you been?" he said.

"Out."

"At the library? That's what you said."

"I'm sorry. Maybe next time you want to chaperone me."

"There's no need to be fresh." He came slowly into the room and stood by the desk, one hand on the chair. "I worry about you, Leslie. That's all."

"What's there to worry about? I was out with my boyfriend. That's what most girls do at my age, isn't it?" I turned my back and started to look for my nightgown in the clutter on my bed. If I started undressing, he'd leave.

"Leslie," he said softly, "I'm sorry. I'm sorry if I've been short, if I've been neglecting you lately. I've had so much on my mind."

"It's all right."

"No, I've been meaning to tell you. I thought it might be nice to spend some time together. Maybe we could go to a concert next week. See what's playing in town. Maybe Wednesday night, after your lesson."

"You have to work, don't you? And Mom drives me to my lesson."

"I could go, instead. I want to speak to your teacher, anyway."

My fists tightened. My nails dug little crescents in my flesh. I shoved aside my pillow, my bedclothes, rumpling everything. No nightgown. Maybe my mother had taken it to wash.

"I don't think that will be necessary," I said.

"Of course it's not *necessary*. It's something I want to do. To make it up to you a little, for all the tension at home."

"Why don't you make up with Steve, if you want to mend fences? He's the one that needs it, not me." And I straightened and turned to face him. "You won't have to take me to my lesson," I said. "I'm not going to any lesson next week."

"Why? Was it canceled?"

"I canceled it." I looked at him eye to eye and saw, with satisfaction, that he was flustered.

"What are you talking about?" he said. "Explain yourself."

"I've decided to take a break. A break from music."

"But—"

"I don't know for how long, yet. Maybe a long time. Maybe for good."

He pulled out my desk chair and sank into it. His face twisted. I could see him trying to collect his thoughts.

"Leslie, I . . . I don't know what . . ."

"I see you're surprised," I said. "But I couldn't really prepare you, it's a recent decision. I only told Elli today. Although for a while I've been noticing my mind wasn't on the music. I couldn't concentrate. I just seemed to be losing interest, you know? And so I thought—"

"You thought? *You* thought? So you're making the decisions now? All by yourself, fait accompli?"

"What's the matter?" I said sweetly. "Besides, I didn't do it alone. Elli and I talked it over. We had a long chat."

"Oh, you did? How nice. But it's me she's accountable to, I'm the one—" He broke off. "She must be going soft in the head to think of such a thing. It's wonderful. The two of you hatching out plans." He got up abruptly and began to pace.

"I'm sure she'd be happy to discuss it," I said. "Why don't you call her in the morning? Have a nice grownup conversation. Two adults."

"Adults is right, miss. You're just seventeen, remember it. You're not on your own yet."

He was fuming. He paced back and forth, raking his

hair, kicking aside any scrap of clutter in his path. It reminded me of the old days, of Steve. But I wasn't cowering in any corner. This was my doing, my game. I was in control.

"You think I can't put two and two together," he muttered. "I've had a lot on my mind, but I'm not blind. I can see the picture, all right."

"What picture? You make it sound like some dark conspiracy."

"Don't be smart. A recent decision, you say? Like I was born yesterday. You think I can't see that you started slacking when you took up with that boy? That friend of yours, what's his name."

"Jeff. His name's Jeff."

"Yeah. Well, when you started going with him, that's when it happened. Suddenly no time to play. Suddenly a million other things on the agenda."

I hesitated. This was not how the script should go. "No, that's not right. That's not the reason."

"That's your story. And I should have stopped it, I knew I should have stepped in before now, but with your damn brother so much on my mind, I thought, well, I'll let it pass. She's acting like a fool, but I'll let it pass. I was soft on you. Obviously, I didn't take it seriously enough."

Suddenly I saw what a terrible mistake I'd made. "It's not Jeff's fault," I said. "It's not because of him. He tried to talk me out of it, to persuade me."

"Good."

"Daddy, it's because of you, don't you see? Because of what you did to Steve."

"Steve? What's this got to do with him?"

But I couldn't seem to get the words out, even though

they filled my head. How angry I was. How unjust he had been. "After Thanksgiving," I faltered. "The way you treated him. Writing him a letter, just throwing him out like that. You never gave him a chance. You never could accept him the way he was. You always wanted to make him over, turn him into something else." I pressed my wrist to my forehead. My head ached. Overhead, I could hear noise; all the commotion had roused my mother.

"Of course, I tried to change him. To guide him. It's a parent's job. But I was always fair to your brother, even this last time. I didn't throw him in the street. I offered him to come home. Three square meals, a roof over his head. It was generous, after his behavior. Leslie, if you don't know, don't talk."

My head was swimming. I wanted to believe him. But that offer of shelter and food—yes, I thought, you'll give him his meals. But no dessert. No Nestlé bars, no sports cars. And I said, in a voice so soft it surprised me, "What was his end of the bargain, Daddy? Tell me, what did he have to do for you?" And looking up, I found myself staring deep into his blue eyes.

"None of it's for me," he said quietly. "It's for him, his benefit. Les: there's no free ride in this life. Not for Steven, not even for you."

He turned the desk chair and slowly, deliberately sat. I wanted to speak, but there was no chance; his low voice had too much momentum.

"Leslie, I know what you think. That I should keep on supporting him, shelling out the money no matter what he does. Just like you think I should look the other way while you run around with this boyfriend of yours. I should stand back and let you carry on till all hours of night, let you neglect your work. You truly believe that, in the fullness of your seventeen-year-old wisdom."

I sat back, flattening my hands on the bed. It was too late, I saw now, to avoid the trap. I was all the way in. "Daddy." My voice shook. "I told you. Jeff's not the reason I haven't played."

"I know what you said."

"But you don't—you can't ask me to stop seeing him." But he could. So easily, he could refuse to let me out of the house. Even deny me phone calls. He could make it impossible for us to be alone. Leave us nothing but the barest encounters at school.

"Les?" It was my mother's voice from the door. She poked her head in and stepped down, looking at each of us, back and forth. "What are the two of you yelling about?" she said. "What is it that can't wait till morning?"

We were both flushed, my father and I, both breathless, and I was perilously near tears.

"Leslie went out?" my mother asked.

"Of course. She just got in. She had such important business, to keep her out half the night."

"It's not that late. She was in by ten-thirty." My mother sat beside me on the bed. "What's going on?" she said to both of us. "What's the crisis?" I didn't speak.

"Why don't you answer, Les? Why don't you tell your mother what you've done?"

Finally, he gave up waiting. "It seems our daughter's quit the violin. In order to teach her old man a lesson."

"I didn't say I quit forever. I said I might."

"It's as good as, Leslie. You stop now, you get out of

shape—what will happen with your audition, then? Life doesn't send so many chances, darling. What will you do next year, if you don't go to school? Sit around the house with your mother, baking cookies?"

A silence. I broke it. "He wants to split us up," I said. "Jeff and me. His punishment. He just can't bear to see me have fun."

"Who's punishing who?" said my father. "You quit the violin to punish me."

"Stop it. Both of you stop." My mother turned to me, lifted her hand to brush away my hair. "Leslie, is this true?" she said. "You've actually given up your music?"

"Well . . . I . . ." Not exactly, I meant to say. Not really quit. It all seemed a lot less clear than it had a few minutes ago.

"How could you do such a thing?" she asked. "How could you even consider it?"

"But it's his fault." I had to make someone understand. "Why is he allowed to twist and manipulate everyone? Only him. Why is he allowed to bully you and me and Steve, and we . . . I . . . don't even have control over . . . over my own . . ." I broke down. A big racking sob shuddered through me and I buried my face in my hands.

"And what did you do?" she asked my father quietly. "What was your response to all this?"

"Very little, I assure you. All I want is for her to stop running with that boy for five minutes. Long enough to think."

"All right," she said to him. She sounded so tired. "Victor, go upstairs, all right? I'll finish here."

Slowly, reluctantly, he turned and climbed the stairs.

My mother got a tissue from the bedstand and wiped my face.

"You've been very foolish," she said. "You provoked him."

"What about what he did to me?"

She shook her head with great weariness. "How could you think of such a thing? Quitting your music. When you know what it means to him. What it means to *you*."

"There wasn't anything else to do."

"Yes, there was. You could act like a grownup. Even if you are only seventeen. A whole houseful of babies I've got here."

I huddled my arms around me. "I should have known you'd take his side."

"Oh, Leslie." She finished wiping my tears and set the damp tissue on the night table. "You're so young. It's all black and white to you, isn't it?"

"Well?" I leaned forward. "Isn't it? Mother, he threw Steve out like old garbage. How can you defend him after that?"

"I don't defend his faults. It was wrong, what he did to Steve. But, Leslie, he's just a man, not God."

"Tell him. He doesn't think so."

"Oh yes, he does. He knows it all too well. You think it doesn't cause him real pain, how badly Steve's turned out? I love my son, Les, but I have to say it, it's true. So far, he hasn't added up to much."

"Daddy's fault."

"You want to blame him for everything. But life isn't so simple, Les. There's two sides to any fight—at least two. Victor's a hard man, but there are ways to deal with him. Maybe Steve could have found a better one than he did." She hesitated a moment before lifting her hand to stroke my cheek. "Leslie. Try to learn from Steve's mistakes. It means a lot to you, your violin. It's not a crime, that your father loves it, too. You're his hope now, Les, his pride and joy. Are you so full of anger that you have to destroy him?" And quietly she climbed the stairs, closing the door behind her.

CHAPTER · 17

THE REST OF THE WEEK passed in uneasy silence. On Saturday morning, my mother made a special breakfast, an onion omelet, which no one wanted to eat. Afterwards, I went down to my room. While I was dressing, there came a knock on the door.

"Just a minute." I pulled down my blouse and smoothed it. "Okay."

It was my father. He pushed the door half-open. "Can I come in?"

I motioned, be my guest. Rather shyly, he entered and stood facing me, leaning his back on the desk.

"I've been thinking," he said. "About the other night, all the things we said. A lot of words came out harsher than I intended. Tempers were running high."

Mom's been at him, I thought. The gentle persuader.

"You mind if I sit down?" He pulled out a chair. I sat on the bed and waited.

"Don't get me wrong," he went on. "I'm not conceding anything. You made some big mistakes, there's a lot of things you don't understand. My opinion about your brother hasn't changed. And about you, too, the way you've been acting. Irresponsible . . ." He broke off. "I had to do what I did, Leslie. I wouldn't be a decent father if I let you go on like this."

I sighed. He'd said all this already. Had he only come to repeat himself? But he seemed to find it hard to go on.

"Les." He ran his fingers through his hair. "About this . . . this Jeffrey of yours. Your mother's been talking to me. She seems to think you'd feel better, maybe be more accommodating, if I let you go out. Have what she calls a normal social life. Me personally, I don't see it that way, but maybe she knows better." How to maneuver people, I thought. How to get them where you want them. Gracefully.

"What did she suggest?"

"Well, a kind of compromise. If you go back to your playing—"

"You'll let me out," I finished for him. He nodded. "I guess that's fair," I said. "But we'd better be clear about it, don't you think? What exactly are the terms?"

"*Terms?* It's not a legal document. It's just"—he searched for the word—"an agreement. We meet halfway. You do your part, and I do mine."

"Yes, I know. But still I think we ought to spell it out. I mean, how often do I get to see Jeff? How many hours of practice for one date?"

"Leslie! What's the matter with you?" He got up and began the caged-tiger routine. Back and forth, back and forth. "When did you start sounding so hard? I don't see that I deserve it, I've never been harsh with you." He paused a moment. "Well, all right, the other night, a little. But you asked for it. And I know what you're going to say: Steve, I'm harsh with Steve. But he's different. I would never treat you the same as him."

I leaned forward, then rocked back, clasping my arms around me. Steve had been so right about it all.

"Leslie." My father stopped pacing and turned to me. He came close and touched my chin, lifting my reluctant face toward him. "Angel. You have such a gift, such a talent. Why can't you rejoice in what you have?"

He would not let me turn my head, so I was forced to shut my eyes.

"Your mother thinks it's best to let you date. And so I'll abide by her judgment. She seems to think he's a nice boy, this Jeff, and how dangerous can it be, a movie or two? But really, I think you know your life lies another way. Another direction."

"Music. Again," I said numbly.

"Of course." He released me. He paced to the window, pushing aside the drapes. "Darling. I know this all seems very important to you right now. Dating, boys. Being part of the in-crowd. That's what teenagers like, to be the same. To all blend in. But you've got to realize you're a unique person. One of a kind. God gave you a great talent that it's your obligation to use. To make something with. You know what I'm saying?"

"Yes."

He paused a moment, choosing his words. "You want

to be grownup, right? Make your own decisions. Well, then, think it through. Where do you want to be in ten, twenty years? And what do you have to do now to get there?"

"But I . . ." I was choking up again. Tears. Stupid tears. "I can't wait twenty years. I want to live now, too. I have to have *some* fun."

"I know, I know." He came over and patted my shoulder soothingly. "That's what your mother said. And so, like I told you, I'm willing to bend. To give in. You see, I still have your welfare in mind. And if you're happier now, then in the long run . . ."

I looked up. I felt so helpless and trapped. I honked into my sodden tissue.

"All right," I said. "I'll do it, I'll do my best . . ." I couldn't finish the sentence.

"Good, Les. You're a smart girl." He patted my arm. "It'll work out for the best, you'll see."

After he left, I spent a long time before the mirror. Washing my face; fixing my hair. My puffy, tear-swollen face looked strangely unfamiliar. Was I pretty? Was I a pretty girl? I wanted it so much, to be pretty. Not beautiful, just good enough. As he said, to blend. It felt so good, being normal. Movies, popcorn. Friends at lunch. How could I think of letting it go?

While I was contemplating myself, the phone rang. It was Bobbie.

"Hey Les," she said. "We're trimming the Christmas tree, you want to come over?"

"Gosh, is it time for that already?" I glanced at the date on my watch.

"I know, it's a little early," she said. "But the kids can't

wait. They're all ready to start unwrapping t.
She paused. "So, you coming?"

"I'd like to. I will if I can."

I went upstairs and slipped on my pea coat.

"Where are you headed?" asked my father. H.
ensconced in his armchair, awash in a sea of newspi .it.

"Just to Bobbie's, for a short visit." I blushed. "They're
trimming their Christmas tree, I told her I'd come. If it's
okay. I'll be back in time to practice." He nodded, returned to his reading. And I walked out, shutting the
door behind me.

The weather was turning chilly. Not snow weather, just
the damp cold overcast we get all winter long here. In
the little gardens I passed, the last flowers were crisp and
brown. The grass had a faded look. I turned down the
walk to Bobbie's house and rang the bell. Even from
outside, I could hear the hubbub. Her brothers laughing,
fighting. Her father shouting for them to shut up.

Bobbie opened the door. "Hey Les." She dragged me
in by one hand and kissed me on the cheek. "Merry
Christmas, come on in. It's like a psycho ward around
here." The tree, a real one, was occupying the better part
of the living room. The oversized television took up the
rest of the space. The floor was littered with ornaments,
boxes of tinsel, tissue paper. An intense piney aroma
filled the air.

"Leslie, sweetheart, how've you been?" Bobbie's
mother came over and gave me a kiss. She seems more
Italian than Bobbie's father, who is. Bobbie's soft bosomy
feeling comes from her mom. I sank into the hug.

"Maybe the last year for this tradition, hmm?" she said.
"Next year, who knows where you'll be."

'It was nice of you to ask me." I'd helped Bobbie with the tree for years. A Christmas treat for a Jewish girl. The closest I get to all that tinsely magic. At first, it was just Bobbie and her mom and me. Then the boys helped. Now it was mostly their show. Ten and twelve, they were still the right age. I watched them argue over a string of lights.

"Come on, they don't need us," said Bobbie, a moment later. "We'll come back when it's done. To admire." She gave one brother a friendly thump on the head and motioned me to follow her to her room.

I climbed the carpeted stairs carefully. Bobbie's room was at the end of the hall. It hadn't changed a bit. Still baby-ribbon pink and starched crinoline.

"God, your family's normal," I said.

"You mean boring."

"No, normal."

She slouched on the bed, her legs crossed tailor-fashion. Remarkable, how graceful she was, plump and sweet. Peaches and strawberries and cream. I sat in a straight-backed chair and rested my hands on my lap. Bobbie so soft. My legs so hard. The difference between us. Between our families.

"Oh, Bobbie." I sighed. "Things are so terrible."

She raised her eyebrows, asking for more. But it was almost too much effort to explain. Downstairs, someone put on a Christmas record, full of bells and chirrupy singing.

She raised her voice over it. "What is it now?"

I gestured, limp. Forget it, let's not talk.

She lay back on the pillow, stretching out, her hands beneath her head. It wasn't fair. Everything was so easy for her. Not the handicap, that was the least of it. But such a happy family. No struggles. Like Jeff, she could go with the flow, ripple along, while I battled upstream, over rapids.

"How are you and Eric these days?" I asked. "Going strong?"

"Okay, I guess."

"You *guess*? Bobbie, don't tell me you're having problems."

"Not exactly problems." She lifted her shoulders and gave a rueful smile.

"Oh, Bob." I sighed. "Why don't we pack our knapsacks and run away? Just the two of us, against the world."

She laughed. "That bad, huh?"

"Really."

It was funny, with neither of us wanting to talk, what pleasure there was in companionship and quiet, somehow, despite the noise downstairs. Quiet within her four walls.

"Bobbie," I said softly, "what's it like for the two of you? When you're together? If you don't mind my asking."

"You mean Eric and me? When we're . . ."

"Yeah. In bed. Or wherever."

She colored, hung back. "Oh, I don't know," she said. "Sometimes better than others. I don't know exactly what I feel about it. Is that weird?"

"I don't know. I'm beginning to think everything in life is weird. Do you . . ." Do you want it? I meant to ask. As much as he does, or more, or less? Who leads and who follows? Or do you decide these things together?

"Do I what?" she prompted. "Do we go all the way, you mean?"

"Well, I wasn't going to ask that, but do you?"

"Twice."

"Was it good?"

"I don't know." She shook her head. "How is it supposed to be?"

"Oh, Bob."

She hitched sideways on the bed and patted the place beside her. I moved over, leaned my head on her well-padded shoulder.

"Life sucks, you know that? It's so . . . confusing." I thought of Jeff. He never rushed me. He was eager, yes, but he never pushed. The other night, I had pushed him. And even then, he had been understanding. To think that I'd almost lost him, through my selfishness and stupidity. My sweet Jeff. Much too good for me. I leaned against Bobbie and gave her a soft punch on the chin.

"I have to go," I said. "I've got my violin to do."

"Let's look at the tree first. The boys will insist."

"Okay." And so we went back downstairs and admired the tree, all trimmed now, with the colored lights flickering and the glitter cardboard star on top. And Mrs. Canelli poured me a glass of eggnog and forced a cookie on me, and I hated to tear myself away, to go back home.

CHAPTER · 18

I CAME IN THE FRONT WAY and found my father's chair empty. He'd gone to the store, probably. And my mother was not in the kitchen. Most likely taking a rest. I went to my room.

What I wanted to do, what I really wanted to do, was see Jeff. Or at least call him and apologize for everything. But I decided to wait. Better to practice first, square that away, so there would be no more friction with my father.

I went to the corner where I keep the violin and lifted the case on my bed. I opened it. And for maybe the thousandth time it struck me how beautiful my instrument was. With its gleaming chestnut color, its scallops and curves. Like a living thing.

I took it out and tucked it under my chin. Slid my fingers up and down the neck, drew the bow across softly.

Tuned up. And waited for that calm, that security which always comes with my practice routine. The long bows, the scales, the arpeggios, every time the same. The sense of dropping into a deep, known place, where time slows. That special concentration. I waited—patient, because it always comes. Sometimes sooner, sometimes later. But every day the same. Except today.

I managed to get through the warm-ups. But I felt disjointed and out of sync. Ruffled, I moved ahead—maybe the arpeggios would be better. I'd done them so often, my fingers knew the way themselves. No need to think, just let them go. But halfway through, memory failed. I stood with the bow in midair and couldn't think what came next. There was just an abyss, a nothing.

I tried to backtrack and succeeded in piecing together what came before. I played it again, faster, a kind of running leap, hoping it would carry me forward past the blackness into the known. But it was no use. I simply couldn't play. The most basic of exercises, and I couldn't puzzle it out.

I sat heavily on the bed, laying the violin on the covers. Nothing like this had ever happened to me before. I felt fuzzy-headed and confused. Maybe I was hungry. Maybe food would help. I put the violin aside and went upstairs to the kitchen. My mother was back. She was making lunch.

"Did you just get in?" she asked.

"A few minutes ago. I was downstairs—" I almost said practicing, but decided not to. "I was at Bobbie's."

"Yes, your father told me. Did you have a good time? How did the tree turn out?"

"The boys did it. We just oohed and aahed."

"You want something to eat?"

"Maybe."

I sat at the table and she put something in front of me, a sandwich, a glass of juice. I ate it.

"Where's Daddy?" I asked. "At the store?"

"Yes."

"What time will he be back?"

"He didn't say. A half-day, I think, he shouldn't be too long." So. Not much time, then.

Suddenly my mother turned toward me. "Leslie," she said, "are you all right? You look a little pale."

"I feel funny."

"I hope you're not coming down with anything." She rubbed her thumb over my forehead. "You're not warm," she said.

"I guess it's just a . . ." I couldn't think of the word. There probably wasn't one. "I think I'll go back," I said. "Start my practicing before Daddy gets home. I . . . I want to make sure . . ." I lost my train of thought. On my way down I remembered that I'd meant to thank her for speaking to Daddy about Jeff. Too late, now; I'd have to tell her some other time.

In my room, all was as I'd left it. The bedclothes were crumpled and messy. The lamp cast a yellow circle of light. Half hidden in the sheets was my violin, still waiting, but I was hesitant now to pick it up.

"Come on, stupid," I said to myself under my breath. "Move already." I forced myself to pick up the instrument and place it under my chin. I tried to compose myself. But I knew before I touched the bow to the strings, just from the feel of it, that everything was wrong. My hands were shaky and my palms were slick with sweat. My concentration and routine were gone. Should I start again from the beginning, do the warm-ups over? I was cold, I probably needed them. But I couldn't quite face them a second time. Not to mention those damn arpeggios. Maybe I should just move ahead, to the music. The Mendelssohn needed work. And so I set up the music stand and opened to the first movement of the Violin Concerto. I stared at the page. And there, instead of the language of music, was a collection of random disconnected dots and lines. Meaningless. As if I'd never learned to read. If I stared hard enough, I could pick things out—a quarter note, an eighth. Dope out the key signature. But not to read, not fluently, as any musician expects to do. It was gone, I realized. To wherever it goes.

This was different, different from my angry resistance a few days ago. Then I had withheld. I was defiant and would not play. Now I could not. The music would not come. And it infuriated me. Why? Why now, when I needed it so much? I felt cheated, and foolish. Like some old senile person, or a silly, fluttery girl, losing her grip in a crisis. All those years I'd invested, learning this wretched instrument. And now when I needed it, for once asked for something back—it deserted me. Of course, it was not a pleasant thing, to play because my father demanded it. But was it such a crime? My mother said I was his hope. So there, I was being a good daughter. Oh, God, I thought. Why has this happened to me? Why now?

Shakily, I reached for the phone and dialed Elli's number. One ring, two.

"Yes?" Thank God she was home.

"Elli? It's me, Les." And without even waiting for the pleasantries, how are you, am I interrupting, I spilled it out. Can't play. Can't read. Do something, Elli. Help me out of this mess.

She listened without interrupting. Then, in her dry way, she said, "Calm yourself, Leslie. All right? This happens, from time to time. It's not an unheard-of-thing."

"*What* isn't? What thing—what's happening to me, anyway?"

"It's a temporary block. You've heard of it, no? Once in a while it happens to people. Musicians, writers, actors. Sensitive souls."

"Wimps."

"What, you think it's laziness? Come on, it's not intentional, right? And believe me, it happens to great ones. Olivier, the actor. And Menuhin, his whole life. Up and down. The gift would come and go."

I sighed. I didn't want a lecture, or a history of the arts. Only an answer. Quickly.

"Elli, please. Spare me. I don't have time for this."

"No? Why not? What's the big hurry, all of a sudden, to play? Last week you wouldn't touch the violin."

"Things have changed."

"Apparently. Still, I don't see the rush. This all started, what? an hour ago? And already you want a cure? Or perhaps, could this have something to do with our conversation last week? And your young man? And your father?"

For answer I gave her sullen silence. "He laid down the law," I said at last. "If I don't play, I don't see Jeff. He'll break us up."

A pause. "Ah," she said at last. "Well. I can't say I'm surprised. I thought he might react this way."

"So you're brilliant. So what? It doesn't make the problem go away."

"Leslie," said Elli after a long pause. "Do you want it to? I mean, do you really want to play? It seems to me that you're more interested in playing games with your father than in playing the violin. I haven't heard once that you miss the music."

And I saw that she was right. That was why the music had gone. Because I'd bargained and dickered with it. Exploited it. Used it—first as a weapon and then as a bribe. In the heat of battle, it had slipped my mind that music has its own life and purpose. I had forgotten all about that, until at last some tiny spark in me rebelled. My integrity—what there was of it. Go on, play your little game, it said. But leave me out of it.

"Oh, Elli," I whispered. And hung up the phone.

I fell back on the crumpled bed. How many years, I thought. How many years and you never failed me: light moods and black, good days and bad. My refuge where no trouble followed. Suddenly I realized what I'd lost. That feeling, that thrill that went deeper than hearing. The vibration trapped in collarbone and chest, resonating. Music in my bones. My father and I had conspired to destroy it. Because we loved it. Because it gave us joy. This ultimatum was only the last interference, the most recent of many. And there was no easy way to fix it and make it right. I could not play. Soon he would discover that and tax me with it: that I had not practiced, had not kept my bargain. Perhaps I had only a few days to stall him, and see Jeff. Barely time to say goodbye.

CHAPTER · 19

THE NEXT DAY, Monday, Jeff picked me up after school and we went for a drive, no place special, down through the back roads, past dried-up corn fields, barren horse paddocks and stabled thoroughbreds, farms changing to neighborhoods, instant houses mushrooming on squared-off lawns. Four in the afternoon and already near dark. A cold, low sky, but no snow. Winter as it always is here—cloudy, waiting, breaking finally into rain and sleet. At last we pulled off the road, into the parking lot of a luncheonette at a crossroads, two stores and a gas station that called itself a town. Jeff turned the motor off and I stared across the street at the shops, the plastic Santas hanging in the windows.

"Christmas is a dismal time to be Jewish," I said.

"When I was little, I wanted to hide out the whole month of December. All those toy commercials on TV."

"I thought you had your own holiday. What do you call it? Hanukkah."

"Oh, that. An afterthought. How can you compare a few dinky candles in a menorah to a Christmas tree?" I gave a dry laugh. "My father used to deck out the store. Hang tinsel and put that white stuff on the windows. You wouldn't think people would buy hardware for Christmas, would you? Nuts and bolts, the perfect stocking stuffers."

Jeff smiled, shrugged. "Well, look," he said. "If you're that broken up over Christmas, I'll make it up to you. I'll buy you seventeen presents, one for every year you missed."

"Thank you."

He nestled his fingers in my hair and tried to draw me closer for a kiss, but I drew back gently. "No," I whispered. "Not now." And I leaned far enough back to look at him. "Jeff. I've behaved very badly. I've . . . sinned, I guess you'd say. Against you, especially. But also against myself."

"The other night, you mean? You were upset."

"That's no excuse." I looked up at his pale face, his intent blue eyes, so eager and sincere. "You were right in what you said, Jeff. I acted like a fool. Practically pouncing on you, and then . . ." I trailed off. "I was angry. Just so angry. After our fight, I went inside and had a fight with my father. I threw it up to him, my not practicing. Taunted him with it, tried to hurt him—everything you told me not to do. And it backfired. He got back at me in just the way I should have known—the way I did know—he would. Through you. He put his foot down. Told me I couldn't see you again, I was grounded. No going out, no phone calls—exactly the kind of thing he used to do with Steve. And the worst of it was—I brought it on myself. If I'd kept my mouth shut, maybe none of it would have happened."

"Leslie. Give yourself a break."

"But look at how I treated you! I didn't think about you, not once. And after all your honesty. All you've done for me." I shook my head.

"Anyway," I went on, "my mother got to work on him and he softened a bit. Said he would reconsider, maybe let me go out again if . . . if I went back to doing what I should. My music." I buried my face. "It didn't seem that bad. You know? I agreed to practice, what was the big deal? I've done it all my life. But yesterday, when I tried, when I picked up the violin—nothing happened. The music was gone, Jeff. Just gone. As if it slipped right through my fingers. I couldn't do it even though I wanted to. Something in me, something deep down, wouldn't allow it. No matter how I tried."

His eyes were swimming-pool blue and shimmering. "So, where do we stand?" he said at last.

"I don't know. In a day or two, he'll figure it out. That I'm still not playing. And he'll clamp down, and—that will be that."

"You mean he'd really punish you for something you can't help? You're trying, aren't you? Can't he see that?"

"I don't know, maybe he can. But it won't matter, he wants what he wants. He punished Steve, didn't he, all those years? For things he couldn't help." Then, slowly, I looked up. "You know," I whispered, "you know the funny thing? I think he really loves me. He even loves Steve, in that cruel way of his. All this pressure . . . He just wants to make me better. Maybe it's human nature to pick and choose and try to change each other. I mean— look at us, Jeff. We go to the movies and stare at those gorgeous faces and then what do we do? We drive home and park and make out in the car. Ken and Barbie on a date. But it's fake. Sort of groping and feeling for the good parts and . . . trying not to look at the rest. At what we really are."

He turned to me then and rested his hands on my knees, on the nylon stockings that covered the plastic that covered the steel. He lifted my skirt and touched me where the stumps of my legs fitted into the plastic sockets, where the flesh was thick and scarred and the heavy straps crisscrossed.

"I'm looking," he said. And for a long moment he studied me in the light.

He started the car then, and we drove toward home. By the time we reached town, it was fully dark.

"You want me to drop you at your house?" he asked.

"No, no, not yet."

"What then?" He touched the brake.

"Pull into the parking lot. Here."

We were outside my father's store. The windows were bright against the evening.

"He still does it," I said. "Look." I held out my hand, pointing to the garlanded window, the sprayed-on snowman. Above the row of stores, the Merchants' Association had set up a plastic Santa, life-size, with reindeer romping on ahead.

"What a lot of make-believe," I said. "All that Christmas stuff. And I used to want it so."

As we sat there watching, my father came into view. He was rearranging the window display, hanging red and green stockings filled with key chains and traveling alarm clocks. His back was bent as he worked, and his wispy hair was blue in the fluorescent light. He worked ten hours each day in a hardware store; it was his life. And I was all his hope.

I said, "To disobey him—to do what I mean to do— will hurt him very much. To choose you."

"Then don't."

"I want to do it." I leaned back in my seat and watched my father work. "I owe him so much," I said. "When no one else had faith in me, he believed. After the accident, when I lost my legs. My mother was frightened. She wanted me to go to a special school, thought I'd be safer. But Daddy wouldn't have it. He made me go out, made me try. The same as anyone."

"Until now."

"Yes. Until you came along."

He fingered my hand in the darkness. "If only . . . if only he could be satisfied. That you're independent. Isn't that what he wanted, to have you go out on your own?"

I shook my head. "His terms, Jeff. He wants it on his terms."

"No one controls that much."

No, I thought. No one does. And I wished for him: Daddy, please. Give it up, let it go. I gazed at Jeff, sitting close beside me. The pale rays of a streetlamp fell across his face, so he seemed to float almost disembodied in the darkness.

"We'll manage," I whispered, and I squeezed his hand. "Come on. Drive me home."

For once, my father returned on time for dinner, surprising in the busy season. He seemed distracted and fumbled with his coat and hat. My mother had made a fricassee of chicken and canned beets and we all passed the serving plates quietly.

Then, as my mother was clearing away, he coughed and said, "I brought you something. Rose!" He called to the kitchen. "Where did you put that box?"

She answered unintelligibly, so he got up and rummaged in the foyer for himself. I could hear the creak of his footsteps, the rustle of crisp paper.

"Here," he said, coming back, arm extended. "It's for the holiday, a little Hanukkah present. I didn't wrap it, you know I don't go in for ceremony."

"Is it Hanukkah tonight?"

"I don't know, one of these nights it starts. What's the difference, anyway? It's just a little nothing."

The gift was nestled in tissue paper at the bottom of a shopping bag. My hand burrowed in, felt softness. "It's very nice," I said, before I saw it.

"Well, probably your mother would have picked something more stylish." He wouldn't meet my eye. "I got it at that store in town. I couldn't get away to the mall."

"It doesn't matter." I pulled it out and, shifting back from the table, shook out the pink sweater onto my lap. It was very soft, angora, with a white lace collar and half sleeves.

"It's very pretty," I mumbled. "Thank you, Daddy."

"Well, you can return it if you want to. I don't expect you to keep it just because I picked it out."

It came into my mind then, as Steve would have reminded me, that I never chose my clothing. It was merely a question of who picked it for me.

"I thought it would be pretty for a party or something," he said. "Your Uncle Al invited us up to his place again New Year's Eve. You know, up in North Jersey. You could wear it there."

"Thank you." I didn't have the heart to say what I was thinking.

I kissed him on the cheek and took the package to my room. In the bottom of my dresser was a drawer full of bulky, seldom-used sweaters. I tucked the new one among the old and closed them out of sight.

CHAPTER · 20

THE NEXT WEEK, the last day of school before Christmas break, I was reading in my room when my father knocked.

"Yes?" I said quietly. I knew the sound of his hand on the door.

He pushed it ajar and slipped softly in. "Am I disturbing?"

"It's all right. Come in."

Stooping a little, he made his way to the desk chair and sat gingerly. "What's the book?"

"*King Lear*. It's for school."

"Ambitious."

I set it aside. Let him beat around the bush, I knew why he was here, what he had to say, why he was reluctant to say it. I could wait.

"Leslie," he said. "Your school break is coming. Right?"

"Yes. Starting tomorrow."

"You have plans?"

"Nothing special. Spend some time with Bobbie maybe, if she's around."

He shifted uncomfortably. "And the boy you like, Jeff. Maybe you were planning something with him?"

"Just hanging out."

That seemed to satisfy him. It wasn't so harsh, to stop us hanging out. Not like dashing plans for a museum trip or a concert. A cultural event.

"I think maybe it would be better," he said, "if you stayed at home. As we discussed." He couldn't even look me in the eye. He grasped his knees with his long bony hands. "You haven't been practicing. Not doing what you promised."

Would there be any point, I wondered for a moment, in trying to explain that I could not do what he asked? That I was not merely being obstinate or sullen?

"Yes," I said. "It's true, I'm not practicing much."

"Why are you doing this?" He crossed and uncrossed his legs. "I spoke to your teacher last week. Miss Rosenzweig. Does she have any notion why you're acting this way? Nothing she talks makes sense to me."

"Yes, Daddy, she knows. She said I was like Menuhin. If that means anything to you."

"Menuhin? He was a prodigy, a brilliant young man, but—"

"He's not young now. He's old, and he's not always brilliant, either. Sometimes, very much. But uneven and unpredictable. The gift comes and goes. Block, Elli calls it. And she says there's a reason usually, if you look deep enough."

"She said all this?"

I let my hands fall limp. "I'm telling you. I figured you'd be skeptical. Or wouldn't see the relevance." Suddenly I was tired of the talk. Wanted it over with. "Never mind," I said. "It doesn't change anything, anyway."

He got up and knotted his hands behind him. "Leslie, you make it sound like I enjoy punishing you. Do you think it gives me pleasure, denying you things? I'm thinking of what's best for you. I can't let you waste your opportunities. With your audition just around the corner."

"All right, Daddy." My voice was almost too low to hear. "There's no need to keep going over it, we've said it already."

"Leslie, I know it hurts. I'm sorry."

"Forget it." I couldn't stand to hear it again: I'm doing it for you, for your own good. I let my head fall back against the wall. "But, Daddy"—I rolled my head toward him—"don't expect anything to change. With the music. Okay? Nothing will be different." He turned sharply and walked out the door.

It was a miserable holiday. Apart from a few visits to Bobbie, I stayed home every day. When I could, when my parents were out of earshot, I called Jeff. He was fine, he said. Lonely, missing me. But patient, which I was not. He said we would get together soon. But I was too filled with longing to wait easily. My mother kept cluttering my time. Now that Daddy had succeeded in locking me up, she kept trying to undo his work. Urging me to go out with her, to shop or visit a friend. Anything rather than sit by myself, reading or watching TV. Over and over I declined the invitations. And at last her resistance wore down and she stopped urging. New Year's Eve approached. She tried one last time to persuade me to come along to my uncle's in Montclair. But I was staunch in my refusal.

"You go without me," I said. "Give Uncle Al and Aunt Ruth a kiss and tell them I'll see them next year." And then I called Jeff and asked him to come. That we would have the house to ourselves.

At eight-thirty on New Year's Eve, my parents left. At nine, Jeff rang the bell. I opened the door and found him, nose red and sniffly, his ski cap jammed over his ears.

"Come in quick," I said. "You look half-frozen."

"It's miserable out. Thirty-two degrees and damp." He straightened his collar and shuddered as he stepped into the warmth. Tucked his hands under his arms.

"Can I take your coat?"

"In a minute."

Gradually he thawed, and took a seat in the living room, perched on the edge of an easy chair. He looked all around.

"What are you thinking?" I asked.

"Oh. Just studying your house. I've never really looked at it, you know. Just been to the door a few times to pick you up."

"In the hall."

"Yeah. And the kitchen." He rested his hands lightly on his knees. It was so strange, talking like this, so formal and proper. As if we had just met.

"It's an interesting contrast," he said. "Don't you think? My place and yours."

"My mother's obsessive. Everything in its place." I sat down on the sofa across from him. "Would you like a candy?" I opened the dish. "We keep a few for display. They're stale."

"No, thanks, not after that buildup. I gather nobody here eats them."

"Not around my father. Although I like sweets." I got up and went to the window. I pushed the drapes aside and looked at the glass beaded with rain.

"I missed you terribly," I said. "I couldn't take it anymore, being alone. One-minute phone calls on the sly."

"I know. Me, too," said Jeff. He leaned back in his seat. "Any developments? With your father, or the music . . ."

"No. Nothing. Except that I haven't tried lately. Haven't tried to play. At first, you know, like when we spoke last week, I fought it. I resented not being able to play. All the trouble it caused. But now I think more about the music itself. I mean—if it were just about him, about my father, maybe it would be better not to play. But—I love it. I miss it. It doesn't seem fair that it should drag on so, this whatever you call it. But I can't do even the simplest things. Even my dumb baby exercises come out all wrong. So now I've started to wonder if . . . if maybe it has to be like this. That to get free I have to give it up. Even though it hurts."

"Hey Les." He leaned across the table and took my hands. "Aren't you overstating things? There's still time, maybe things will get better."

"Maybe." Then I had a sudden thought. "Jeff—would you like to hear my piece? The Mendelssohn concerto? Not me, I mean—a tape. I have Heifetz doing it, that's my favorite version."

"Where?"

"It's in my room."

He followed me back through the kitchen and hesitantly down the two stairs. Then I remembered. He'd never seen my room before.

"Oh," I said. "I forgot. It is strange, isn't it. It used to be a den."

He paused on the last step, looking around. And my eyes followed his, from the flowered coverlet on the studio bed to the thick drapes to the rows of cassettes on the bookshelf.

"You have a fireplace in your bedroom?"

"It doesn't work. At least, no one's ever tried it."

He came down and sat on the edge of the bed. "Isn't it awfully dark?"

"Well, it's nighttime. But you're right, even during the day it's gloomy. There's only one window, and those heavy drapes. Plus the door to the back yard, but I don't use it much." I sat lightly beside him on the bed, just so, and we let the stillness settle on us.

"Oh, the music," I said, remembering. "I was going to put the concerto on for you." I loaded the cassette and pressed the button to start. Then I sat on the desk chair facing him. For a moment there was just the scratchy noise of an old recording and the faint hiss of the tape. Then it began: the violin's abrupt, sweet, searching voice. Jeff sat in rigid concentration, trying to understand something new and unfamiliar. And as I watched him, it was as if I heard it myself for the first time. I had played it so often, disassembled it to nuts and bolts and put it together again, note by measure by phrase. I had heard it played by half a dozen masters. How had it never struck me before, Mendelssohn's boldness, his impatience with chitchat? How he plunged in, full of urgency, speaking his mind from the first note. No time to waste. And that theme! Poignant, they say, piercing the heart. And so it is, shot forth, the very arc of an arrow. I listened to Heifetz play, razor-keen, and through him, the perfect medium, heard Mendelssohn's lyric voice, bare and unafraid. Heard his shining candor. His openness. Courage, he said to me. Leap. Take it in your hands. Make it your own.

I got up, too restless to be still. I went to the door and closed it, went back to stand near Jeff. Sat. Stood.

"What's the matter?"

"That music. Do you hear it?"

"Of course I hear it."

"But do you hear how . . . how . . ." What was the word I wanted? Fearless? Bold? "No wonder I couldn't play," I said. "I was afraid. Guts. Jeffrey: I didn't have the guts." I sank beside him on the bed; I was shaking. I touched my fingers to his leg. "That day in the car," I said. "When you raised my skirt and looked at me—Jeffrey, that's what it's like to play. How it has to be. Naked. No safety. All alone. And to come out, to let people see you. Jeff, it's not enough to be fair. To give the music respect. You have to give all. Without reserve. Everything."

He opened his mouth to speak but did not. And I moved toward him and touched his throat above the collar.

"Are you sure?" he said; I nodded. We undressed and lay together on the bed. And I looked at him, thin and frail, with narrow bones and raucous red hair and white skin. Tight spastic legs and penis upthrust between them.

Himself. Not ugly or beautiful, but there. And his parts, not good or bad, but of him. I lay beside him and he touched me, the soft places and the scars, the pink plastic and straps and hinges. And he eased them from me. We pulled back the covers on the bed and lay between the smooth sheets, cool and slippery at first but then warming around us.

"I don't know," said Jeff, after a long time, "how far you want to take this. Whether you're ready."

"Yes. I am. I want to."

"Les—you understand, it's not necessary."

"For me it is."

I held his hands tight, his knuckles pressed painfully between my own. Words were not strong enough to carry what I felt. If I gave all I had, it would not repay him for what he gave me: myself. But myself was all I had to give, so I said, "I'm ready."

"I'm not sure *I* am." He hitched up on one elbow and reached for his pants. "I came prepared. You know, Boy Scouts. Just in case." He fumbled and dropped a packet of condoms on the bedstand. "I may not know what I'm doing, but I know I wouldn't want to hurt you."

"Thank you." And so we went on; we helped one another. It was not easy, to nest our imperfections. As he entered, there was a moment's pain, a burning stretch, but the pain was less than I feared. We moved together, rhythm and synchrony, things I knew. And after, as he lay quietly beside me on the bed, I looked about at my room. All was familiar, every paint chip and thumbtack hole. All belonging but Jeff, misplaced in this otherwise mapped-out and totally known world. And I realized then it had to be here, in this place where I had clumsily penciled my third-grade reports and played with my paper dolls and practiced hour upon hour on the violin, it had to be here in this place that I became myself. And I buried my face in his shoulder and felt his arm around me, and the smell of his body was good, the smell of both of us together.

CHAPTER · 21

THE NEXT MORNING, I rose early in the quiet house. I had been asleep when my parents returned, Jeff long gone. A late night for them; now they would sleep late. And the silence would be mine to fill. I opened the case and took out my violin. Caressed its narrow waist and slender neck. Its beauty. And began to play my long bows, seeking that perfect rich sonority. My old routine; but the voice newly imagined. Created fresh in my mind.

I had worked through the warm-ups and on to Bach when my father came. Charmed by the music. I let him in.

"Leslie. You're playing."

I nodded. Shut my eyes. Deeply stroked, bow to strings.

"It's good to hear," he said. "I knew you'd come around. I knew you couldn't leave it for long."

And I stopped and set the instrument carefully on the bed. "No, that's true, I can't," I said. "I love it." I sat on the bed; I was still in my nightgown. "It's not how you think," I said. "It's not because you punished me. Locked me in."

"Punished you? All I did was give you a little breathing space. Time to reconsider."

"I saw Jeff last night," I said. "Here at the house. I asked him to come."

It caught him unprepared. For a moment, there was confusion in his expression, then anger.

"How . . ." he faltered.

"I took advantage of your absence. I was . . . determined."

He pulled out the narrow desk chair and crumpled into it. His hand passed through his hair, teasing it up into a white plume. "Why are you telling me this?" he said. "I would never have known."

And I thought: openness. "I wanted you to know," I said. "That I won't give him up."

He was no longer able to restrain himself. Suddenly he jumped to his feet and paced the room, his arms clasped across his chest. To the window, gazing out. And back.

"For God's sake, Leslie," he muttered. "Why? A gifted, talented girl like you." He shook his head. "It's not even so much that you defied me. That, you already did. But why do you want to throw yourself away? On . . . on a . . ."

"On what? On a cripple? I love him, Daddy. Though I'm not sure I deserve him."

"Love? What do you know about love?" For a moment

he struggled to control his voice, find his words. "You think in a few years of living you could possibly understand such complexity? Love is a slow thing, a nurturing. Not a fun time, a date. A drive in the car." He rubbed his forehead. "Leslie. Do you remember, after the accident? How bleak it was? And nobody, not you, not your mother, not your brother, ever thought you'd amount to anything. Beached. You just lay there on that couch. It was only me. Am I right? I was the only one with the faith, the foresight. Who kept on telling you to try. That's what love is, not—" He broke off in disgust.

"It always comes back to that," I said softly. "Always. The music."

"You're gifted, Leslie. I was doing my best by you. And now—now some boy comes along, looks your way, asks you out for a malted milk, and in one minute you forget everything. Your work, your parents, your standards, everything. Right out the window, just like that."

"You make it sound like a betrayal. Like something I did against you personally."

"It might as well have been. You threw away everything I gave you." He shook his head. "This business of refusing to play. How else should I take it, if not as a rejection of me?"

"And how should I feel? That if I don't play, you don't love me?" I studied his back, his ropy neck, the wingbones angling out beneath his shirt. "Daddy. I know you love me. But why can't you grant me some respect? I wasn't holding back to punish you. Well, at first maybe, but not after, not . . . Daddy, I couldn't play. I wasn't able. At least, not till today." I felt myself flush as I said it.

"Pah." He spoke to the curtain. "It's nonsense. I don't believe it, Leslie, all the romantic claptrap—the great artist, everything so mysterious. It's a craft, that's all. You work hard, you practice, you do the runs over and over, and you play. All the rest is hype. And if nothing comes out, you're not trying enough. You don't care, your heart's not in it."

"How do you know?" I shook my head. "You tidy it up so nice and neat, but how do you know what it's like to make music?"

"I've lived a long life."

"But you're not an artist. You're a hanger-on, a stage mother. All right, you love it, I'll grant you that. But you don't play the violin. I do. Don't tell me where the music comes from, because you don't know. Even I don't know: it *is* mysterious. And you don't know everything about love, either." His muscles were tense, his shoulders high. His knobby back to me.

"You say you love me," I went on in a low voice. "Fine, all right, I accept that. It's your kind of love. But what makes you so sure about Jeff and me? Is it because we're kids—seventeen, eighteen years old? Or maybe . . . maybe what bothers you is that we found each other on our own. That it wasn't something you planned."

He turned. And he seemed so fragile and old, with his unruly white hair. "Oh, Leslie," he murmured. "Leslie, you're a child, an infant. If it wasn't so pathetic, I'd laugh."

"At what?"

"I don't want to say."

"What makes you want to laugh? Me?"

"Not you." He let his head fall back, stroked his hair.

"Sweetheart. There's so much I never wanted to say. Like when you were a little girl, playing dolls. Pretending things that never . . ." Slowly he turned his gaze to me. "Leslie, this boy. You think he loves you?"

"Yes."

"Loves *you*, Leslie?" His voice was achingly weary. "You know what he wants, don't you? Can't you guess what a boy like that is after?"

"Sex, you mean? Why don't you say it, then: it's the twentieth century. Daddy, you sound like something out of a Victorian melodrama. You know, I . . . I feel things, too."

"I know, Leslie, I know you do, that's the point. That you are so willing, too willing. Just to have a boy notice you, bring you a box of candy, you would . . ." He tossed his head. "And don't tell me it's not like that, that it's different, a new generation. Boys are the same. I know what they're like, believe me, I was a boy myself. They can tell when a girl is easy prey. They don't waste any time jumping in."

For a moment silence, like a fine snow, settled on the room. "Because of my legs," I said at last. "You think this because of my legs."

"Not think. Know. *Know*."

I searched out his eyes, forced him to meet my own. "But it isn't . . . wouldn't be like that with Jeff. Jeff is like me. We're the same."

"Angel. Sweetheart. That makes it more true. That kind of boy, excuse me, a cripple, who else—"

"Who else would have me? Is that it?" I shook my head. My eyes wandered to the violin beside me. "And his?" I said. "The music—what was that for? Your way of making it up to me, I suppose. For what I lacked. What I couldn't have."

"I wanted to protect you. That's what I wanted all along, to shield you from being hurt."

"But in this? In music? Daddy, don't you know it's the last place to hide? That music—art—is naked. Bare. Wide open." My face was hot; I pressed my hands to my cheeks. "You always wanted me to play for people, to perform. But I never could. Because there was risk. The risk of being seen, of failing. Daddy, can't you see that without courage . . . oh, Daddy," I whispered. And could not go on.

He turned his back and climbed the stairs. And I reached out and touched my violin, ran my fingers over the honey-colored wood. I could no longer hate him, or feel anger. Only sadness, that even love could not be perfect.

CHAPTER · 22

IN FEBRUARY, on the bitterest day of the year, Steve came home. He rang the bell and stood waiting outside like an encyclopedia salesman, shivering with cold, dressed only in a canvas jacket and chinos. My mother opened the door and saw him there and for a moment she was nonplussed.

"Well, come in," she said. "You'll catch your death."

It turned out he had no warm clothes; they were in storage in the closet upstairs, where no one had thought of them.

"You've been going around like this all winter?" my mother asked, taking a handful of the thin cotton. "Why didn't you buy something decent?"

"I didn't have the money," he said simply. He batted

his hands against his shoulders and then sat on the couch and opened the candy dish.

My father put him to work at the store. Steve did just well enough to stay on. He overslept routinely, but not so much as to make him late for work, only for breakfast; he was always running out of the house with a cheese Danish in one hand. He got a haircut. But there was still a trace of sloppiness about him, something too trivial for Daddy to take issue with. The shirt not crisply tucked in. The high-topped sneakers. The faint blond stubble on the baby-pink cheeks.

He was pleasant, even respectful to my father, but evenings he kept to himself. I wondered what he did up there in his room alone. Reread old comics? He didn't want to talk about his months of exile; didn't talk to me at all. The only time we spent together was in front of the TV. But I didn't sense any anger from him. That was burned out.

One Saturday, I climbed the steps to his room. It was so long since I'd been upstairs in this house, I felt a bit lost, like a tourist overseas. Steve's door was shut, but I knocked a couple of times and he finally answered and let me in. It was just as I remembered, cluttered with high school knickknacks, the bed wildly rumpled—he'd always been an athletic sleeper. I had interrupted him in doing a puzzle, one of those little black rectangles with the letter tiles that slide around to make words.

"Not working today?" I asked.

"Every other Saturday off."

"Want to go out for a drive?"

He gave me the merest glance. "Not particularly," he said.

"I thought you loved to drive."

"It's too cold to put the top down. Damn car's drafty even shut."

"It couldn't be chillier than this house, could it?"

He shrugged, and then, obliging me, rummaged around on top of his desk for his keys.

"I'll tell Mom," I said.

We drove, where else, to the shore. A couple of people were walking dogs by the water's edge. It was low tide, the beach was heaped with seaweed and broken bits of shell.

"You wouldn't think you could pollute a whole ocean, would you?" I said, resting my elbows on the boardwalk rail. "All the garbage washing up now. Medical waste. Syringes. Nothing's clean anymore."

Steve dug his hands in his pockets. How odd, I thought. He's still wearing that cotton jacket, even now, with a wool coat in the closet at home. The tip of his nose was bone-white, but red splotches, like thumbprints, marked his cheeks.

"Are you home to stay, Stevie? You really back for good?"

"Why not? I don't have anyplace better to go." He reached inside to his breast pocket. Found a joint.

"Want some?" he asked.

"No, thanks."

He lit it. "You're not going to give me any motherly, disapproving little talks, are you? You'll let me be?"

"No. I'm done lecturing. It's your business." But I reneged immediately. "You really should get out of here, Steven. Out of the house. You're killing yourself."

"Killing myself? Isn't that a bit of an exaggeration? I

was a lot more likely to die when I was on my own. Of malnutrition. Or exposure or something. Like one of those bums in the park, begging drinks." He inhaled deeply. His eyes watered. And it struck me then how Steve had changed over these months. The devil-may-care was gone. The boyishness.

"Was it hard for you?" I asked. He shrugged. He had a lungful and wasn't ready to talk yet.

"Fairly," he said at last, letting out the smoke. "Well, you should know, you told me."

"I kept hoping I was wrong."

"No, no such luck, pet. You were right, as always. Shit jobs, high rent. Just like you said."

"I was wrong about other things," I said. "About you." And I wanted badly to hold his hand, but didn't. "You could make it, you know. On your own. If you wanted."

"Your faith is touching, Les. But honestly I think you've got me mixed up with someone else."

"No, Steve. You're smart. And if you'd only stop wasting your energy, fighting . . ." How? I thought. How to convey it? He turned his hazel eyes to me. They were filming over, losing focus as the high came on him. "You've got to stop proving stuff," I said. "Stop reacting. Trying to be good or bad, to fit him . . . Do you know what I mean?" His gaze wavered. He blinked. "Step out of it," I said. "Just quit the game."

Maybe he was too stoned to think now. Or perhaps it was a step he wasn't ready for, or never would be. For all his mistakes, my father had bathed me in love. A lifetime's worth. While Steve was still looking for crumbs, always scrambling, never catching up. Perhaps he would never find the courage to step free. I glanced at him from the corner of my eye. He probably resented me, too—that I did as I pleased now. Set my own course. While he was forced to toe the line.

We walked down the promenade, toward the spot where Jeff and I first touched. And I thought: What a long process, love. And not over yet. There, on the sand, I felt it first. Desire. Heat. Only later, warmth. Acceptance. That mighty stretch.

Soon it would be spring, my audition. I was working very hard, but there was so much to learn. Like a baby, in a way, starting over from the beginning. Creating it as I wanted it to be. Work was a deep pleasure. Then summer would come, and fall. Jeff and I would leave for college. And already I missed him, ached in anticipation. Perhaps he would meet someone else and leave me. Or I might leave him. Fall in love again. Perhaps, despite my work, I'd fail my audition. Or maybe I'd get into school, be a great success there, only to find that no one outside wanted me. I'd end up a second-string in a third-rate orchestra. Or . . . well, who knows? No end of disappointments the world can dish out. But I would be ready for them, arms flung wide to gather them in and feel the sting.

Because my father was right. He wanted to shield me for the simple good reason that life is full of pain. He knew that if I opened myself to love and joy, sooner or later someone—not Jeff maybe, but someone—would reward me with a hard boot in a soft place. And he wanted to shelter me from that. But the cost was too high. The shelter too unbearably lonely.

I took my brother's hand and tugged him toward a bench.

"Let's sit a little and watch the waves," I said, seeing he was not fit to drive. And so we looked at the sea. The foam lapping, the flat packed sand. The gulls crying and dipping overhead. How beautiful, I thought. I'll just stay awhile and take it in.